# Winter Willow

DEBORAH-ANNE TUNNEY

ENFIELD
&WIZENTY

Copyright © 2019 Deborah-Anne Tunney

Great Plains Publications
1173 Wolseley Avenue
Winnipeg, MB R3G 1H1
www.greatplains.mb.ca

Great Plains Publications gratefully acknowledges the financial support provided for
its publishing program by the Government of Canada through the Canada Book
Fund; the Canada Council for the Arts; the Province of Manitoba through the Book
Publishing Tax Credit and the Book Publisher Marketing Assistance Program;
and the Manitoba Arts Council.

Design & Typography by Relish New Brand Experience
Printed in Canada by Friesens

Library and Archives Canada Cataloguing in Publication

Title: Winter willow / Deborah-Anne Tunney.
Names: Tunney, Deborah-Anne, author.
Identifiers: Canadiana (print) 20190110406 | Canadiana (ebook) 20190110414 |
    ISBN 9781773370255 (softcover) | ISBN 9781773370262 (EPUB) |
    ISBN 9781773370279 (Kindle)
Classification: LCC PS8639.U56 W56 2019 | DDC C813/.6—dc23

**ENVIRONMENTAL BENEFITS STATEMENT**

**Great Plains Publications** saved the following
resources by printing the pages of this book on
chlorine free paper made with 100% post-consumer
waste.

| TREES | WATER | ENERGY | SOLID WASTE | GREENHOUSE GASES |
|---|---|---|---|---|
| 5 | 410 | 2 | 18 | 2,250 |
| FULLY GROWN | GALLONS | MILLION BTUs | POUNDS | POUNDS |

Environmental impact estimates were made using the Environmental Paper Network
Paper Calculator 4.0. For more information visit www.papercalculator.org.

Canadä

FSC
www.fsc.org

MIX
Paper from
responsible sources
FSC® C016245

*For André*

The compensation of growing old, Peter Walsh thought, coming out of Regent's Park, and holding his hat in his hand, was simply this; that the passions remain as strong as ever, but one has gained—at last!—the power which adds the supreme flavour to existence—the power of taking hold of experience, of turning it round, slowly, in the light.

VIRGINIA WOOLF, MRS. DALLOWAY

# I

I cannot remember my thoughts as I looked at him sitting behind his desk, no longer living but a corpse. And that's one truth to be told about what happened that night. What I remember clearly though is that I was alone for only a few minutes before the scene was disrupted by others—Celeste, the housekeeper, who knew the moment she saw him that her life would never be the same, and then the officials, starting with the police, the paramedics, and finally the coroner. They crowded the room with their questions and suspicions. But before they arrived, in that moment with silence drifting down like light from a far source, I was alone with Stone, my tormentor, my saviour, my strange love.

◆ ◆ ◆

Earlier in the evening, the night had come in cold to this house called Winter Willow. It settled darkly with a hard determination in the two massive floors above where I stood. I'd seen it hours before as I was packing alone in my room—I'd seen the sky grow dull and then in its familiar fragmenting, turn dark. And now this dark, cascading down the elaborate staircase from the second floor to the first, mixed with the weak overhead light from the hall lamp, lingering in corners, on each stair, the window ledges, and in the vestibule with the beautiful crystal etching of a willow tree.

. . .

The series of missteps that led to my being in that ornate room began on the day of a general meeting of staff and graduate students at the university where I was a PhD candidate in English literature. It was 1976—a time I look back on with a complicated longing for how I lived then, alone and unencumbered.

At seventeen, when I'd received a scholarship to attend university, I moved away from home and left my mother in the city where I'd spent my childhood. Our apartment was on a street of low-rise apartment buildings, red-bricked, in the middle of a series of streets, parking lots, passageways and back alleys. I have no doubt that after I departed, the voices and screams from the children playing in the cluttered yards and adjacent fields continued to enter the modest rooms of our apartment, continued to barrage my mother as she went through her day without me. I see still the chesterfield pushed tight against the wall, a matching moss-green chair against the adjacent wall, a small reprint of Tom Thomson's *Lone Pine* on the wall beside the front door. This painting is now in the upstairs hallway of my own home and on occasion when I pass it I think of it in the living room of the apartment where I grew up.

My mother had died ten months before the day of the department meeting and after her death I was in essence alone. An only child, my father long gone; I never knew the story of why he left and really never wanted to. I know to some people this would seem strange, but my mother and I had been a team since I was young and allowing anyone else into that tightly knit union would have seemed to me a form of betrayal.

My thesis on London after the First World War focused on writers such as T.S. Eliot, Virginia Woolf, and Katherine Mansfield. So intense was my study that I came to see them in the faces of people on the street or the bus. I had come also to assume the mood of 1920 London, a mood I likened to pale light on linen, to passageways smudged with fogged shadows. And overriding these imagined places there was a poignant disillusionment, extending beyond the heavy-bricked dwellings and hallways with their lingering smell of onion and fried meat, to the very air I breathed.

Being poor suited me. I was fine with it, as I was with being alone. I liked it even. From my mother I inherited a large rose-coloured chair that extended to an almost prone position and at night, in my room, I'd read there, enrapt by the texts, and content to be alone. I'd sometimes sleep in that chair, with thoughts from those books circling the room. Reading had always been a comfort, like pulling a thick blanket over me, something warm and sleep-inducing, while outside it would be storming.

I loved those long stretches of quiet, the meditative quality of studying, its removal for a while from everyday concerns, such as money, relationships, or for that matter, the future. I wonder now why I was so attracted to this sedate life, my ambition limited to my studies, to obtaining a degree, to later teaching. The death of my mother hung heavy over me; I see that now. And my life of contemplation and study, a threadbare existence, was one I came to value and to see as the only way I could cope at the time.

But all this was to end the day of the English Department meeting, that cold January afternoon, the first day after our Christmas break. Standing at the back of the conference room with a crowd of my colleagues, I thought how I hated those gatherings and braced myself for the inevitable boredom.

The department head, Professor Warren, a man in his late sixties with large earlobes, the skin of his scalp dappled with age spots and wiry grey hair pulled tight in a ponytail, stood before the podium. "It is my unpleasant task to tell you of cuts to our budget," he said looking up at us and glancing down quickly, assured that this statement had fastened our attention on him. "Funding will be cut next term and we will have to reduce the number of classes. A committee will determine how best to go about this." He looked up again, caught my eye. "But immediately the writing assistance program will be cut." This was my office and I was the only person who worked there. I saw other graduate students shift to look at me and one who had been standing close by moved back slightly, as if my bad luck could be contagious.

My scholarship had stopped the year before, and although I lived frugally, I still needed money for rent and food. As the department head spoke, across the room I saw my academic supervisor, Professor Edison , a solid, squat woman with helmet-styled black hair, so shiny that her head looked wet. I saw too the slightest flicker of a smile and remembered at our last meeting she'd said my thesis was bordering on being unoriginal and was taking too long to complete.

When Professor Warren was finished speaking and everyone was leaving the room, I approached him by the podium, as he crammed papers into his portfolio. Before I could speak, he said without looking up, "Sorry about this, Melanie".

"But my funding was dependent on that program."

"I know. But you must be almost finished. I mean, can't you graduate this term?"

"No. Last fall I completed the comps, but I still have the thesis and its defense."

"What's it on, again?" I knew he was trying to move our conversation to a less contentious topic.

"Early twentieth century British literature."

"Yes, I remember now. Your advisor mentioned it." He looked back to his briefcase, snapping the buckles shut. "So how long do you think?"

"A year, year and a half."

"Well, you can do it part time, I mean work, and complete the thesis at night."

It struck me then. They didn't want me here. They thought my work inferior. This sudden thought stung, and I could not speak. If I worked on my thesis only at night it would take years longer and I would be out of academia, putting my best energy into a job. And what job would that be? I'd worked as a secretary one summer in a government office and never fit in with the other secretaries, women who looked at each other when I spoke and who stopped asking me to join them for coffee breaks after the second week. The men were just as mysterious—bloated, jovial men who spoke loudly, filling the office, hallways and cafeteria with their commanding voices.

When I left the room, Professor Warren was still speaking, advising me to look at the bulletin board in the administration building, where there were job listings which, he said, might be appropriate.

◆ ◆ ◆

When I came to the university, it was to be the graduate student of Professor Coburn, the scholar I had read during my undergrad years. He was an expert on D.H. Lawrence and was known in the faculty for his compassion, for the hesitancy of his speech, and his careful use of language. He spoke with a stutter, as if his thoughts were so plentiful that they jumped over each other, after which he'd take his hand, large and wide, and sweep it across his face. I came to know when he did this that I should listen closely, that what he was struggling to say was complex and crucial.

He spoke about the influence of the First World War on the literature that followed, in the 1920s. "How could it be otherwise?" he said one day when I had joined him in his office. He was at his desk, fiddling with a paper clip, looking toward the ceiling.

"What do you mean?" I said.

"The war was horrible, of course, but it was mostly horrible because it was such a shock. The barbarity of it, and most of those men, the men in the trenches, had no idea that life could evolve into such horror. Living with fear so profound and long stretches when nothing happened, only to be punctuated by death and the worst sort of living conditions. It marked them. It marked the whole generation."

"And the women?" I said. "The women didn't go into battle."

"I know, I know," he said. "But they were of the time and many of them had a role to play in the war. They felt the sorrow, they saw its fallout, would probably notice it more clearly than the men." He straightened his back, let the clip fall to the desk. "What did

Katherine Mansfield write about Woolf's novel *Night and Day*, that it was a lie in the soul, because she did not deal with the war? Oh, they knew, they saw what happened, how the men returned broken."

After this explanation, he was quiet, but I knew if thoughts had physical substance, the room would have been crowded with them. "How could they not know that *fear in a handful of dust?*" he said without looking at me, but then shaking himself back into the room where we both sat. "No, Melanie, it wasn't something only the men would have known." He gestured at the bookcase across from him. "Over there. See those books. Bring them here. I don't want you to read criticism, or at least not yet. I want you to read these, they'll tell you about those years, what happened, how for so many people the world closed in."

The books he recommended depressed me. I read about the soldiers, their fear, the lack of hope, the way death was a constant and I had no doubt it changed them, so that when they returned to their lives it was with the dread and hopelessness that permeated the era itself.

When I'd meet with Professor Coburn in his office to discuss my reading of the war and the heart-weariness it brought with it, he was often distracted, sometimes muttering, his face bright with elation or dark from confusion. I came to love this distraction. He'd sit before his bookcases, staring above me at the ceiling, his fingers a tent of contemplation, quoting Eliot or Pound, speaking of the strife writers from this era knew, and how they were able to alter into art what they'd seen and felt.

"Here, here," he extended yet another book. "Take this, think about it. We'll talk next time about democracy after the war, how so much of what we see today is a direct result of those times." The day he gave me this book on the war, and I accepted it wearily, was to be the last time I would speak with him. I wish now that I had paid closer attention to what he said, to how he looked and how he looked at me. But instead I rushed from the room, a touch annoyed at having another book on the war to read for our next meeting.

# 2

Less than a year before the day of the department meeting, while I was away in the city where my mother was in a hospital, Professor Coburn died in that room where we had so often sat speaking of the literature we both loved. He had a heart attack or stroke, I'm still not sure which, but I knew he would have been, at the moment of his death, utterly surprised by the betrayal of his body—a surprise that would have been greater than his pain or fear. I know this because he always seemed so oblivious to his physical being.

Within two months, my mother also was dead, in her case from breast cancer, and when I returned to the university, I was assigned Professor Edison as my advisor. I'd seen her over the years and knew that our area of study overlapped, but I had never spoken with her and had no desire to, so cold was her demeanor toward me.

From the beginning we did not work well together. My mother's death, mixed with the trauma of Professor Coburn's death, created in me an interlude when I felt removed from my studies and from life generally. In the library, in the small cubicle office I'd been given in the English department, or in my space at the rooming house, I would often stop reading, a finger marking my place, and stare into the space around me, not even sure what I was contemplating. I see now that the two deaths, so close together, stalled me, so that I was unable to venture beyond these places I had come to know as home.

. . .

My mother had always been the constant of my life and because of that familiarity, seldom considered. She was like the sky above me, the returning seasons, or the rooms of our apartment which were so known as to be thought of merely as home.

The years I attended high school, she and I usually stood together waiting for the morning bus at the corner of our block, a neighbourhood of apartment buildings and townhouses. One day I noticed I was nearly as tall as her, with the same straight back, and my hair the same strawberry blonde.

She worked for many years, until her sickness made it impossible, as the office manager of an insurance company, a position title vague enough that she was tasked with all aspects of keeping the company afloat. It was a family-run business, and I met the owner, Mr. Mendelson, only once when I went to the office to pick up our apartment key. He was grey-haired, trim, and I estimated about twenty years older than my mother. When he saw me he said, "So, this is the Melanie I've heard so much about."

"Yes, my daughter," my mother said, coming out from behind her desk. "She's lost her key." She reached me and turned me around so that I was facing the door, pressing the key into my hand. As my mother did this, he leaned against the desk and watched us, a smile just beginning to pull his lips back. Moments before, I'd been told by the receptionist where my mother's office was located and when I reached it, I'd barged in expecting to find her alone. Now, standing between the two of them the thought struck me that I had disturbed a private moment, for a sense of intimacy seemed to linger in the room.

When I was leaving, feeling rushed and strangely unwanted—something I'd never felt with my mother—he said, "You're one lucky girl to have this woman as your mother."

At home, later that day, I asked her why she was anxious for me to leave when I was in her office and she said, "I was busy, that's all."

. . .

Although we did not have much money, my mother always wore
tailored, expensive suits to work, even during hot summer months.
She owned three, one navy blue, and two grey and with them she'd
wear either white- or pastel-coloured blouses, with nylons and high
heels. Her hair was worn in a twist at the back of her head, and
every morning she applied pale foundation, mascara and peach lipstick, makeup that served to create the look she was not wearing
any makeup at all. Her voice was quiet, measured, and she exuded a
calmness that precluded raucous or what she considered distasteful
talk. If a conversation threatened to veer toward such a topic, she'd
turn her head, perched on her long neck, and look away.

. . .

Across the hallway from our apartment lived a family of five children,
two sisters and three brothers, who moved in when I was thirteen. I
befriended the youngest girl, Joni, and when I'd visit her apartment,
I was amazed by the noise generated by her family. I could always
tell which room the three boys were in by their loud jostling and the
sound of their laughter. They looked similar, with dark cropped hair
and bodies that displayed an angular vitality, so that I came to think
of them as a single, destructive force, like three Dobermans, who
were always acting in unison. Her parents were tolerant of the noise
in a way I knew my own mother would never be. In fact they'd add
to the chaos by speaking in commanding, loud voices which were
never heeded. I suppose I especially enjoyed her home because it was
in such stark contrast to my own.

After a month of visiting them daily, one morning when we were
getting ready to leave for the day, my mother asked, "Can you tell me
what your attraction to our new neighbours is all about?" She was
standing in our small galley kitchen, curlers in her hair, toast starting to burn, and as she grew more and more angry, I watched her
mouth, outlined with peach lip liner, opening and closing, sharply,

as I imagined a bird would peck. This was the first time I stopped and watched her with still, critical attention, critiquing her movements, her clothes, what she was saying. "Why, Melanie—why are you going there? These people are not like us," she said, flicking the lever up and quickly flipping the toast onto a plate. She shook her head as she buttered each slice.

We could have reached out our arms and touched the cupboards on both sides, so narrow was the room. I was caught in the space between the wall and her, unable to escape. Smoke from the toast filled the small area. "I do everything for you. Everything. And what do you want to do? Hang around with a bunch of hoodlums." She kept her head down, cutting the toast into angry squares.

. . .

Joni shared a bedroom with her older sister, Angie, who saw Joni as an annoyance, and who complained if she came into the room and found the two of us there. I remember an afternoon when I was fifteen and Joni and I were rifling through her sister's clothes. We were looking for something Joni could wear to see her boyfriend, who was picking her up within the hour. He and his friends had been working all afternoon on an old car he'd bought for less than a hundred dollars, and Joni was excited to be going out in it. "We'll probably go to the drive-in, the one out by the airport." She quickly shoved the T-shirt she had contemplated wearing back into the drawer when we heard Angie's voice in the hall and knew she was headed for the bedroom.

"Oh no," Angie said when she entered the room, "what are you guys doing here?" She took out a pair of jeans from the closet that Joni had been eying and accused her of wearing them.

"Those? Are you kidding?" Joni said. "My ass isn't as big as yours, I'd never fill them."

"Nothing is big. You're a skinny little rat person. But I swear if I find out you've worn anything of my clothes…" She let the threat dangle as she shifted through the hangers in the cupboard.

After she left the room, Joni gave a low bow to the door and we both laughed. "I can hear you," Angie said from the hallway, and then, "Little losers," under her breath.

Hidden under the dresser was Angie's makeup bag, and Joni dragged it onto the bed. There we experimented with eyeliner, shadow, lipsticks. "What do you think?" Joni asked after she outlined her eyes in black and applied a pale pink lipstick. She looked different, older and tougher. "My mother would kill me," I said.

"My mom would not care." Joni reapplied the lipstick and rubbed her lips together, viewing her face from one side and then the other in the mirror over the dresser.

•  •  •

Why does this day come back to me so clearly? The day I felt my friend was in some fundamental way leaving me behind, driving away in her boyfriend's old Studebaker, dressed in her sister's suede jacket. That Saturday night, after Joni had left with her boyfriend, I went back across the hall to my own apartment and spent it watching a movie with my mother, each of us at either end of the chesterfield, not speaking, until the credits rolled and my mother stretched and stood. "Now, that was a good movie," she said. "Please turn off the lights before you go to bed, will you dear?"

I sat there after my mother left and felt the deadness of the room, the weak light from the overhead lamp, the way everything I could see remained static and fragmented with dark as the night came in. Eventually I did stand, turned off the lights and made my way to my small bedroom where I lay awake most of the night wondering what Joni and her boyfriend were doing.

•  •  •

My friendship with Joni was the only real issue of contention I remember having with my mother. I think of that now, I think how I could call Joni, who still lives with her husband and children in a farm fifty miles outside the city of our childhood, and even though our lives veered in opposite directions with her marrying young and having children, it would be mere minutes before we'd be making each other laugh. I think too of how when my mother died, it was Joni who came to the apartment to help me dismantle the life my mother and I had lived there. When I was emptying a kitchen cupboard, I came upon the cup my mother used every morning for her coffee all the years I could remember, and when I looked at it in my hand, it seemed inconceivable that it could still exist, and she did not. Unbidden, a sound came from my throat, and Joni dropped what she had in her hand and came over, wrapping her arms around.me and the cup. We stood like this for what seemed an immeasurable amount of time. What would my mother have thought, I wondered, if she'd known that my only source of comfort after her death had come from the friend she found so unsuitable.

# 3

Shortly after the meeting of the English department and after I spoke to Professor Warren, I went to Professor Edison's office. She did not move from behind her desk and looked at me over her glasses. "Guess this means you'll have to speed up that thesis," she said, glancing back to the papers in front of her.

"But what about TA work? I could help with grading," I said.

"No, I have everyone I need, and by this time so does everyone else in the department." She was still not looking up and so I was able to evaluate her, a heavy dark clump in front of me, her black suit strained across her shoulders, the squat round face that held the hard marbles of her downcast eyes. As I did this, another student entered the room and she looked up to him, smiled as she accepted the files he passed to her. "Is this all of them?"

The man was tall with thick, honey-coloured hair and a look, when he glanced at me, of barely suppressed amusement, as if he were concealing a joke. Both of us stood before her desk, but she looked only at him. "Yes, they're all there," he said.

"Good," she shifted through the papers.

Before he turned to leave he faced me, lifted his hand and said, "I'm Martin Mackenzie. Sorry to hear about the closing of the writing program."

"Melanie," I said and took his hand. He held mine longer than I held his, but distracted, I turned back to face Professor Edison.

"You should check out financial aid," he said. "They may be able to help."

"All right, Martin. That's all," Professor Edison said turning her attention toward me. "Well, I think the only thing you can do is finish by term's end. You can always continue at night, you know, while you work somewhere."

I was hot and growing annoyed. My long hair was stuck in the collar of my coat and the sweater I wore—a grey loose weave sweater I'd knitted over the Christmas break—was making me perspire and feel confined. "But I can't. You know that. Term's end is only weeks away." Finishing would have meant completing my thesis, which I had only started to plan. Two months earlier I'd completed the comprehensive exams, and since then I had concentrated on rereading primary material and finding supporting secondary sources.

"Maybe you should have thought of that before," her voice trailed off as she picked up a pen and began to write as if I had already left the room.

· · ·

At the administration building, I checked the bulletin board, then went to the second floor to the financial support office. There an officious-looking woman with grey hair sat at a desk behind the counter and looked up at me with pronounced boredom. After retrieving my file and opening it on the counter between us she said, "You should be finished by now." She shuffled through the papers. "Or almost."

"I'm just wondering if there's any way this office can help, financially I mean," I said as she twisted her head to read comments on the file.

"Well, I wouldn't think so." Her eyes were pale blue and resolved and her gaze quickly slipped over me. "No, sorry," she said shutting the file. "There's really nothing we can do."

· · ·

It was the first week of January and had been clear and sunny since Christmas, so that the snow on the street and sidewalks was packed hard as white cement. *How long can I survive?* I wondered leaving the admin office and walking out to the street. I had never felt so fully alone as I did on that day, holding my collar against a gust that whipped across the intersection, ripping the coat from my hand. I twisted to catch it—the cold wind extreme as a slap.

The day was darkening as I walked the two miles home, numb with a feeling similar to the grief I felt after the loss of my mother. Loss begets the memory of loss, I thought. By the time I reached the concrete bridge that crossed over the river, the sky was dark and falling snow shimmered with fragmented light. Streetlamps shone through the storm, round and pale gold, the slant of snow reaching into the distance where the string of lights receded and dimmed.

I lived on the outskirts of the city center, part of an area called Rosemount Hill, in an old house that had been converted to rooms or bachelor apartments. The neighbourhood was made up of streets of large houses, facing each other along roads of huge oak and maple trees that had been there so long their boughs interlaced.

My room only had space for the lazy-boy chair that had been my mother's, a single bed under the window, a small washroom in what had been a closet, a large wardrobe, squat refrigerator with a hotplate above, and piles of books. I could see the entire space from my chair, which I found comforting.

In a vestibule between the front door and the hallway of my rooming house, there was a row of metal mailboxes with the names of each inhabitant on tiny slates of paper. The mailbox with my name written in dark ink, Melanie Schofield, was beside the mailbox of Elsa Bennett, a woman I estimated to be almost fifty years older than me, who occupied the room across from mine and who appeared to live with little support or contact outside her home.

When I arrived at my rooming house that day, Elsa was in the hallway. "Oh Melanie. There you are. I've been worried." She believed she had a clairvoyant gift and would often state her opinion as if it were a fact.

"I'm fine Elsa." As we spoke I was struggling with opening the lock of my door. "Just fine."

"Do you want me to help?" she asked just as it unlatched. Elsa was tall and thin, on that day wearing a red vest with embroidered beads along the edge, a black chiffon dress in ruffles, the hem of which touched the heavy construction boots she'd inherited from her father. She had applied red lipstick to her mouth with a clumsy touch, so that red leaked into the thin lines of her upper lip and was smudged beyond her bottom lip.

. . .

After I was able to unlatch the lock and enter my room, standing with my back to the door, I thought of Elsa and the Christmas that had just passed. I had spent it alone, the first since my mother's death. Waking that morning, I looked out to the sidewalks and street, empty and laden with a heavy covering of snow, and the view had seemed a form of absence, a silence solidified. I spent the rest of the day reading Henry James. It's not that I did not have an option, for some of the graduate students who did not have family in the city had planned a dinner and I'd been invited through an announcement left in my mail slot in the English department. My plan originally was to join them, but I kept putting off confirming my attendance and as the day wore on and I thought of all that was happening across the city, of children opening gifts and dinners being prepared, things my mother and I had done on Christmas day, I was glad I'd not responded. It seemed being alone was somehow a fitting way to mark my first Christmas without her.

That evening Elsa had crossed the hall and knocked on my door. I made her a cup of tea and gave her one of two muffins I'd bought as a Christmas treat. We sat speaking of Christmases when we were young and before she left she sighed heavily and said, "And look at

me now, Melanie. Alone, and so many of those people gone or dead."
She stood then, stretched. "And the ones still here, living not that far
away. Strange how life unfolds." And without looking at me, she left
the room, leaving half of her tea and muffin behind.

• • •

In my room, I thought of Elsa on that Christmas evening, of her
sudden sadness, which the next day was replaced by her usual high
spirits when she crossed the hall once again to give me an angora
throw. It had been her mother's and she would not leave until I
accepted it. I could see that throw now, in a square on the back of
the rose-coloured lazy-boy. I glanced at the other items in my room,
one by one. Despite their meagerness, I felt a protectiveness toward
them, a pang that they could be lost, in fact that they inevitably
would be lost. I fell on the bed, pulled the blanket over me and slept,
waking at nine that night. The lights from the street shone weakly
on the ceiling and I watched the shadow from the sway of the huge
oak before the house, the only movement in the dark room. I knew
I had to get up, eat something, think rationally about what I would
do, but instead I lay quietly, turning every so often to see the time
and realize another ten minutes had passed without escaping the
paralysis of the day.

At almost ten o'clock there was a knock on the door, followed
by the sound of Elsa's whisper, "Melanie. Melanie. Are you there?"

I stood, stretched and stepped to the door, opening it to the
dimly lit hallway and her anxious face. "I'm sorry, dear," she said.
"It's late I know, but I need to talk to you." Elsa was often the only
person I'd speak with in the building for weeks. And although I was
fond of her I also knew her perceptions were not to be trusted, that
she had a litany of enemies, from the janitor to the mailman—a sour,
unspeaking person whom she was convinced was bringing infection
with the mail. Once when I picked up my correspondence from the
front hall, she whispered to me, "… hell itself breathes out contagion,"

nodding toward the mailman who was by then on the pathway lead-ing from the house.

"What is it, Elsa?"

"It's you. I've been thinking about you all day. I'm worried."

"About what?"

"The forces that are gathering."

"It's all right. I'm fine. Really."

"But I'm worried."

Then I did a curious thing and I did it without thinking. I lifted my hand to her cheek and cupped it for an instant. "Don't worry, Elsa. I'll survive."

# 4

Over my years at university, I had come to love the walk to get there. It started on streets lined with houses like the one where I lived, buildings which had been renovated into boarding or rooming houses. From my street I'd cross the bridge with its concrete pillars and high round lamps, which in the evening illuminated the sidewalk with a pale gold light. From there I'd move to streets that widened and where birch, large oak and maple trees leaned over the yards of houses that had stayed single-family dwellings. These homes were imposing, many far enough back from the road and enclosed by fences and hedges that I was unable to see their front entrances. They always fascinated me—those large three-storey homes lining the street, the side arbours twined with rose vines above stone pathways, and the elaborate porches and verandas, some with pillars and doors made of heavy mahogany or oak. In the evenings, on my way back to the rooming house, I'd walk those streets, with the sky dark blue behind the houses and gold light filling the rectangles of windows, their bulk brooding and mysterious. During the day it was unusual to see anyone on the grounds except gardeners, and the buildings themselves were so formidable that it seemed to me the lives they enclosed must also have been grand and unknowable.

On my way to the university, I was contemplating how much easier those lives were than mine, in fact how much easier money would make life, when I noticed an open side gate that led to a large garden. The early morning fog had not burnt off and thick rolls of white mist roamed the ground where I walked. Against the sky, whipped with clouds, this handsome mansion extended out in spots into the fog. It was built of grey stone, with turrets jutting out at the corners, a white porch extended along the front façade with a high staircase of wide steps joining it to the yard and stone path.

On a whim, and feeling hidden by the fog, I followed the path along the side of the house into the back yard, which was divided into separate gardens encircling a central pathway and fountain. Snow covered the low bushes and dead flowers, arbours were laden with ice-encrusted vines. The abundance of snow and cold created a sense of abandonment, as if it were a place once loved but now forgotten. Low bushes and the husks of dead flowers bent by the snow gave a lumpy appearance to the garden, their bulk like white animals nestled in sleep. The sky dropped a frosty web and the somber scene before me seemed infinitely sad. Once that sensation began to overtake me, I found reason for it—my mother's death. The ghostly silence of the place, beautiful though it was, brought me back to that grief as I moved into the furthest reaches of the garden.

When I looked up from my thoughts of grief and beauty, I saw a man standing before me on the path. There was no chance of hiding from him for his expression told me he'd seen me. "Who are you?" he asked. "I don't know you." It was as if he was questioning himself, as if he did in fact recognize me. Tall, white-haired, he had a face that had, no doubt, been pleasant, maybe even handsome, but was now closing in on itself. "What are you doing here?" his tone turned from inquisitive to angry as he came closer. "Did you come here to steal from me?"

"No, of course not," I said, his question provoking my anger so that I answered indignantly. "I just saw the gate open."

"And you thought, what? You could just come in here?"

My instinct was to apologize but his tone spurred me to contrariness. "Is that so terrible? That I wanted to see the garden?"

"My garden, young lady, and yes, it is terrible. You are trespassing." His eyes were darkly alive and angry beneath his bushy eyebrows. "Besides, it's winter, what did you think you'd see back here?"

Now I too was infuriated, not just at the situation, for I knew I was in the wrong, but at all that happened to me in the last day. "Exactly what I saw. The garden is beautiful in winter, and what makes you think that other people don't deserve the chance to see it? What makes you so special?"

"You silly girl, do you not know who I am?" he said. "I am Stone Shackelford."

After a moment's silence, I said, "I've heard of you. You're the writer." My anger forgotten as I recalled his novel, the one he was most known for, and I was silenced to think that its creator was standing before me. I'd heard he lived in the city, near the university, but did not know he lived this close or that most days I had passed his house. The book he was best known for was written more than fifty years earlier, after the First World War, and as I searched my memory for the name, it came to me: *The Uninvited*. I remembered too it was the title of a frightening movie from the '40s, one I watched with Joni in her apartment, while her brothers, in an attempt to frighten us, snuck up behind the chesterfield, jumping out at the most suspenseful moment. But this movie had nothing to do with Stone's novel. In fact, all I could remember of the book was there had been a love affair which ended sadly, but how or why was lost to me.

"I read your book when I was seventeen." When I said this I remembered where I'd read it, how my mother leaned against the door frame to speak to me, a finger pulling at a ringlet of blonde hair that curled along the collar of her shirt. These memories crowded in while he watched me, while a silence seemed to extend from us and settle in the garden. Was it the sadness of the novel's story, its tale of loss and regret, that evoked the image of my mother at that moment—my mother as she had been before the illness struck, on a common Sunday afternoon as I read in my room?

I saw his pale blue eyes—or would they be considered grey? All I knew with certainty was they matched perfectly the silver-grey yard and freezing air, and that they were alert with agitation. I decided it was best to leave as quickly as possible.

"Don't worry," I said. "I'm leaving."

"Not so quick." His tone softened. "What led you into my garden?"

"I pass your house every day on the way to the university. I'm a PhD student there."

"You looked so thoughtful when I saw you here. You didn't even hear me approach," he said.

"I was thinking how sad and beautiful this garden is, and how even more beautiful it must be in spring." Why did I say this? I look back and wonder. Perhaps it was that the setting—the chilled air, frosted bushes, the dead flowers caught in fog, and the white light of early day—all served to quiet, so that it was a moment in which it seemed only the truth was fitting.

He turned from me, looked toward the sky, and said after a few moments, "Yes, it is, but then spring does not always come." Beside him was a gardening shed, large as a guest house, and close to me was a willow tree, laden with snow; it looked brittle, and its branches drooped in the fog. I touched it and he said, "That's the name of this house."

"What?" I said.

"This house, it's called Winter Willow. My mother named it." He looked back to the sky. "She was an artist and sketched the willow tree, so it became the house's emblem. We had it etched in the glass of the front door."

Another moment of silence yawned between us until he said, "Come into the house. I'll show it to you."

. . .

We entered the house through the back door, which led to a porch with frosted windows and large wicker chairs, abandoned in the winter cold. Beyond the porch, through a double door, was a large but poorly lit kitchen. There were two stoves, a massive refrigerator with glass doors, a low chandelier that cast a clouded light over the room. A woman, standing by the sink, turned when we entered. "Celeste, this is…" then he turned to me, his outstretched arm asking that I provide my name. She was short with blunt-cut hair, yellowy grey, her eyes pale brown and although her appearance indicated she was in her sixties, her movements were quick, and she gave off an air of someone disturbed, compelled by an unspecified agitation.

"Melanie," I said offering my hand, which she ignored.

"Hello, Melanie," she said turning back to face the sink and dipping her hands into the sudsy water.

"Celeste, the side gate seems to be open."

"I'll see to it, sir," she said, her back still to us. To me it seemed I'd entered another era, an era where people referred to their employers as 'sir'. Their exchange suited the room we stood in, with its high ceiling, framed by wide mouldings and on the floor, thick baseboards. Its formality spoke of the type of order that was aligned with privilege. What I did not know then was that I was never to hear her refer to him as 'sir' again. The kitchen cupboards were painted a pale yellow and the walls an off white. Long cracks, like etches, spanned the ceiling, the faucets and taps were old and scratched, and the overhead lamp smeared a dull light over the room.

"Come with me, Melanie," Stone said, leading the way to the front of the house. He brought me into the large vestibule where we could see the massive front door, mahogany-framed, with a panel of glass and crystal, etched with his mother's design of the willow tree. Crystal triangles framed the image, and as sunlight began to cut through the fog of the street, a faint prism fluctuated on the wall behind him. "Beautiful, isn't it, and completely unique."

"Yes," I said. Seeing the street now mostly cleared of fog, I felt an urgency to continue my walk to the university.

"Follow me, please," he said and entered the large room to the left of the vestibule. There I saw huge bookcases lining three walls, with a tall ladder on a roller that could move between them, allowing access to the top shelves. He sat behind the desk, before the window where light poured in plentifully. In my coat and boots, I stood in the middle of the room, looking toward the window and seeing a halo of blinding light which outlined his form. Books were piled on the floor, circled the desk where he sat—some along the wall, some under the curtains, which puddled on the hardwood, some haphazardly placed in the bookcases, most leather-bound and many dust-laden.

"Sit," Stone said, pointing to the chair before the desk. "You say you are a student at the university?"

"Yes."

"And you were on your way there?"

"Yes."

"But I sense there's something wrong," he said, his fingers splayed together before him.

"Yes," I said. Looking back I wonder why his statement did not surprise me, instead I told him about losing my position and my need for employment. Watching the interest he showed while I spoke, I thought he might know someone at the university, someone who could help with my attempt to find a position.

He opened the top drawer of his desk and took out a pipe, lighting it with the lighter he found on the mass of papers before him. He took two deep puffs and looked up to the coffered ceiling. So smooth was his glance over me that it seemed I had become part of the room. "You look like someone," he said after a few moments.

"Everyone says I look like my mother," I answered. I was becoming hot and annoyed at waiting. I opened my coat, removed my scarf and held it in my lap.

"Put your coat in the hall," he said.

"Mr. Shackelford," I said, leaning forward. "I really should be going."

He interrupted me, "I said put your coat in the cupboard in the hallway," as one would speak to a willful child. I stood, took off my coat, stuffed my scarf and mitts in its sleeve and left the room. And now I wonder why I did not leave, why instead I listened to him, hung up my coat in the vestibule and returned to the library. He watched from behind the desk and when I sat down he said, "Where do you live?"

"Not far, on Fairmount Street."

"And you need a job?"

"Yes."

"Well I was going to say I need an assistant, someone to arrange this library, answer correspondence, that sort of thing."

"I could do that." I heard the eagerness in my voice and knew, by the way he looked down at his desk, he'd heard it too.

To deflect from my enthusiasm, I stood and walked around the room. "Your library looks amazing."

He picked up his pipe again. "Tell me about yourself," he said after a few moments. I was standing by the bookcase, leaning my head to the side in order to read the titles of the books. I chose an old leather-bound copy of Thomas Hardy's, *Tess of the d'Ubervilles*. It had long been one of my favorites and I remembered when I was growing up at home there had been an old paperback version with a torn cover. My mother had loved British writers and we had all the novels by Hardy. "I'm afraid there isn't much to tell," I said. I was leafing through the book, settling on passages. Then, looking up, "I need to finish my doctorate and then I'm hoping to get a job teaching."

"But losing your funding, doesn't that mean the department thinks you, I don't know, that you are unworthy somehow?"

I shut the book. This had been my thought too, the conclusion I'd come to while lying in bed the night before. "Not necessarily."

"Have you considered it could have something to do with the way you present yourself?" he said.

"What do you mean?" *That's a weird thing to say*, I thought as I put the book down and returned to the chair before him.

"You must know that. I mean that you're beautiful."

My mother had been beautiful. I knew that. And I knew that I looked somewhat like her, but I had never considered myself beautiful. A boyfriend in high school had said it to me once and at the time I thought it sounded a little too adult to be taken seriously. "Well, I'm just saying the way you look, it doesn't always make life easier, as some people think."

"So?" I said not understanding why he was telling me this or what it had to do with my working there. "The job?"

"Yes, I could use you," he said, leaning back in the chair. "But you need to sign an agreement that you will not share anything about what happens in this house."

"What?" I said, and then, "Why?"

"Because people want to know what I'm doing. What I'm writing in particular." He asked me what I'd been paid at the university and when I told him he said he'd pay the same. "Fair?"

"Yes, fair," I said. "Some days I could come in the morning, but usually it will be the afternoon. Is that ok?"

"Yes. You can come on weekends too, whatever is convenient. I'll have the paperwork ready." I gave him my name and address and when I stood to leave, he stood also. "Take that book, the one you were looking at, take it as a gift."

"Oh, no, I couldn't."

"Yes, I can see you loved it and that will make us friends, Melanie."

He smiled then, his eyes shadowed by a wide forehead and those thick eyebrows. Under the overhead light he looked skeletal, thin to the point of gauntness, and haunted in a way I should have noticed. I would see him like this often in the coming weeks, but this first time, when he spoke directly to me, his eyes alert, the skin creased around them, I wondered what he saw when he looked at me, a young woman, captive in his gaze. While he was calculating, deciding somehow on the role I would play in his world, in contrast, I was aware only of my relief and gratitude.

"I'm tired now," he said. "I normally do not see people so early in the day."

"And I should be off."

"Before you go, I'll ask Celeste to show you around." When he left the room to find her I was alone. A thick swath of light from the front window streamed through sheer curtains into the large room, lighting the desk where Stone had just been. There was something in the quiet way the room settled that made me sleepy.

He returned with Celeste, who said, "This way," formally and I followed her to the back of the house. "The kitchen," she said simply. "This is where you will usually find me. My rooms are off here," she indicated a door beside the glassed-in porch.

"Nice," I said.

"Yes, it's a nice old house."

"Bit like him, I guess." We were in the narrow staircase leading from the kitchen to the second floor and she stopped, forcing me to stop as well.

"What are you saying? He's a great man, a great writer."

"Well, yes of course, I know."

"Do you?" she said, and before I could answer, "You can reach the upstairs floors by this stairway," as we mounted the last steps and entered the second-floor hallway.

"But I think I'll only be working on the first floor."

"You'll need to know where the bedrooms are. There are days when he does not leave his sitting area." I could tell she was becoming annoyed with me, her voice strained and rushed. In the hallway, we were greeted by a coldness as if a door to the outside had been left opened. "We don't heat the rooms we don't use," she said. "It would be a waste and he hates waste." Although a small woman, I could see she was strong and what my mother would have referred to as feisty, sure in her opinions. "This is his room," she said standing by one of the doors without opening it. Beneath the door a line of light filtered into the hall. "No doubt, he's in there now, so we must be quiet." Moving further down the hall she stopped at the next room, "This is the second-floor library". As with the first-floor library, books were strewn everywhere, papers scattered on the desk. In this way the room had settled into a comfortable disarray.

"The second-floor library," I repeated. "Imagine. Is there a third-floor library too?"

"The third floor is not used. There's nothing up there." She turned to me and in the dull light of the hall, I could see the lined softness of her skin, like moth wings. "It's one of the reasons it's colder here. We never heat the third floor."

I was cold, rubbed my hands together, but Celeste ignored my discomfort. "And here," she said before reaching the front staircase, "is your room."

"Oh no, I don't need a room," I said, and Celeste shut the door without speaking. "I already have a room," I said following close behind her. "I'm only working here, there's no need for a room." She walked ahead of me and remained silent.

# 5

At times, studying in the university library would take on a meditative quality. I'd be reading about the time between the two World Wars, and the mood of the era would infiltrate not only my impressions but the sounds of the room itself—people walking about, closing books, dragging them off tables, the sound of voices that either whispered or could be heard muffled in the stairwell. These sounds amalgamated when I could see how night would come to streets in 1920 London. How, in poverty, poets, philosophers and their families survived on scraps, on gruel, on a diet of the cheapest food. The dinner smell of stewed onion and meat would linger in the rooms and hallways of their apartments. In my imagining I was there, could sense their desperation, smell the mixture of food and wood burning. I'd see children and dogs in alleyways, a baby that could be dead in a month crying long days in a cold room.

Those soiled streets where men walked, their dark clothes too thin to guard against the insistent cold, their boots with holes making their socks soggy and frigid, and their faces closed in on the heavy task of their routine. In their minds a shapeless despair from the memory of the war formed, its purple-skied evenings, its mud and fear. I sensed it all, the waste of lives settling behind the doors of townhouses and squalid apartments while fog spiraled and coiled along the dirty-cobbled streets.

These lives long lost were there when I'd read, or at night before falling into sleep. I was able to sense them, alongside my own life, with its small, closed rooms, its grief, its mounting darkness.

. . .

After meeting Stone, and being in Winter Willow for the first time, and after spending the rest of the day in the university library, reading a biography of Katherine Mansfield and John Middleton Murray and being unable to concentrate, I returned home to find Elsa in the front hallway. She was pacing and looking up to the ceiling. "Such beauty, there's such beauty," she said and when I asked her what she meant she replied, "I can see it coming and it makes me happy." It was not unusual for Elsa to have such sightings, or visitations, as she called them. I took her hand and led her to my room. There I made tea for the both of us. As she sat in my one straight back chair by the small table where I ate, smiling and rocking back and forth, I told her about my new job. Taking the teacup in both hands as if the heat was providing comfort, she said after a loud, noisy sip, "What would your mother think?" It was a strange thing to say, for she had never mentioned my mother before and normally I would have dismissed it as one of her ravings, except that the same thought had struck me walking home.

. . .

Restless and unable to sleep that night, I imagined telling my mother about meeting Stone, about what had happened to me that day. I realized, lying awake and looking at the ceiling, that she, or rather the memory of her, was moving away from me in some fundamental way. She was becoming static in my mind, set in the way she'd been when I was a child and no longer able to advise or comment on my adult life. But then I too had no clear thoughts regarding how I felt about Stone, other than relief, tempered by a nagging sense that all was not as it seemed.

◆ ◆ ◆

The next morning, after having my tea and toast, showering, dressing in my usual winter attire of black leotards, a patterned skirt and
sweater that either I or my mother had knitted, I decided I would
spend the day at Stone's. That way I'd have a better feeling of what
would be expected of me. Edgy from a dream I'd had where I was
stuck in a dark closet and could not find the door handle, I felt a
weary apprehension.

On the front steps of Winter Willow, I rang the bell. The etched
glass image of the willow tree that Stone's mother had created was
lit by the clear winter sun and through it I could see Celeste enter
the vestibule and open the door. By way of greeting, she said, "You
should come in the back way. That's where I usually am." There had
been no change in her expression of resigned boredom when she saw
me, and I knew she was thinking that my coming here was going to
be something she would have to endure. When I entered the house,
the hallway felt cold. "Put your coat here," she pointed at a closet
under the central staircase, not the large closet in the vestibule where
Stone had told me to put my coat the day before. I was reluctant to
give it up for it was so cold but thought doing so would make me
seem ungrateful or judging. "Stone is in the first-floor library," she
said, turned and walked toward the kitchen.

When I entered the library, he was lying on the leather couch, a
throw over his legs, dressed, as he'd been the day before, in a suit, tie
and vest—a 'get-up' as my mother would have said. When he looked
up at me, I could see him clearly, the strain across his forehead, his
sallow skin, and estimated he was in his mid to late eighties. "So you
decided to come early," he said, and before I could speak he added,
"I've been thinking, you should live here. We have so much room and
living here would save you money."

"Oh no, I have a place of my own."

"A place in a rooming house is not a home," he said.

"But it can be."

He looked at me as if what I was saying was inexplicable. "All right, suit yourself." He went back to reading his book, and without looking at me said, "But remember there's a place for you here."

The idea of living there between those two strange people who I imagined rattling around in all that space seemed unappealing, but I replied, "Well, thank you, Mr. Shackelford."

He looked up again, "Stone," he said harshly. "Call me Stone."

♦ ♦ ♦

I spent the day taking books from the bookcases, dusting and stacking them in adherence to Stone's complicated sorting system. "I'm keeping North American literature down here, the rest in the second-floor library. Except, of course, for my own books. They're separated. And my contemporaries. I want us all together." The books had been stacked and placed in the bookcases in no particular order, some bound in soft leather were old and had belonged to Stone's parents, but most were first editions purchased by Stone over the years.

His British contemporaries were writers I knew well from my studies: Forester, Eliot, Lawrence, among them, and when I'd sort their books, I always stopped and took a moment to read a passage. During my first week there, I picked up and started reading *Howards End*, when Stone entered the room, catching me, engrossed and crossed-legged on the floor. "So, Stone, you must have read this when it first came out," I said. "This is a first edition."

His look softened from the inquisitive and strict expression when he first entered the room. "Yes," he said, walked to his chair behind the desk and sat down. "Yes. I bought it in London when I was there."

"You were in London in the 1920s?" Oh, how interesting, I thought, that this Canadian writer had been there and influenced by the same forces that influenced the writers with which I'd always felt the deepest connection. And I wondered if it was possible that he could have known what I merely imagined.

"Yes. After the war. I stayed there, in London."

"So, the early '20s, you were there?"

"Yes, didn't I just stay that?"

"But you see this is the time I'm studying. I think I mentioned it. I'm fascinated by this era. Did you get to meet anyone there?"

"Of course I met people."

"I mean writers. Did you meet, for example, Virginia Woolf? Oh God, how I would have loved to have met her."

"No. And I never had any desire to either. I couldn't be bothered." In my excitement I had missed that his tone was growing annoyed.

"But you were writing. You were a writer at the same time. Didn't meeting them interest you?"

"I wasn't there for that. I met my first wife then." He shuffled through the papers on his desk, not looking at me. "It was a somber time, really quite bleak. The war and all."

"I'd love to speak to you about the war's impact sometime," I said. "It might even help with my studies."

"Do you think that's why you're here?" His sharp tone surprised me, and I straightened. "You think I want to relive those unpleasantries so that you can have information for your schoolgirl studies?" He stood, looked down at me, his face shadowed with antagonism. "I'll be upstairs working. Don't disturb me."

# 6

When I returned home the following evening, after having spent another day at Winter Willow, I was greeted by Eve, one of the few students who lived in my rooming house whose name I knew and who I would stop to speak with if we met by chance. She was rushing to class but with a breathless urgency told me that our rooming house was being sold and its tenants were to be evicted, or at least some of them. "The new owner wants to keep those people living on the second and third floors to pay for the building," she said. "He's going to live here, so I think the rooms on the first floor, like yours, will not be rented." *And Elsa's,* I thought and then wondered, even before I wondered about myself, where she would end up.

"While you were out, he came here. Spoke to each of us and quickly had his rooming house full." She took her bike from the pile of bikes leaning against the wall of the hallway.

"Totally full?" I asked. This news, after the elimination of my funding, left me feeling freshly under attack.

"Well, I haven't decided for sure to stay, but yeah, I think everyone else agreed to remain." I watched Eve hoist her bike into the vestibule, then carry it down the veranda stairs. "Be careful out there, it's slippery," I called after her as I thought how quickly things change. This thought gave way to the idea that it now made sense to move in with Stone, and I knew I'd have difficulty justifying, even to myself, the rejection of his offer. And still it was against my better judgment to move to Winter Willow.

◆ ◆ ◆

Although the next day was a Saturday and I had slept poorly, waking every couple of hours to lie placid and worry about where I would end up, I decided to work at Winter Willow for the day. Going there, I reasoned, might help to clarify if I should move there or not.

When Celeste answered the door to me, she said in a rushed voice, "I hear you have to move."

"And how did you hear that?"

"A neighbour." I had never seen any neighbours, much less any who Celeste, who spent her days indoors, would speak with, and I wondered, in any case, which neighbour would know about the sale of a rooming house a quarter of a mile away. I removed my boots, placing them on the plastic tray kept at the door. "Will you come here to live?" she asked, and when I did not answer she followed me to the front hall where I hung up my coat. "I mean it makes sense, if you have nowhere else you could go." I glanced at her mildly and walked around her to enter the library, returning to the pile of books I'd been sorting the day before.

"So I guess it makes sense now for you to move here." She stood in the middle of the room watching me move the books from the floor to the desk where I could sort them more easily.

"I like my solitude," I turned the book I was holding to read its spine.

"Solitude in this house is never a problem."

"Why do you care, Celeste?" My voice took on a sudden, harsh tone that surprised even me as I shifted my gaze from the book to her.

"He'd like you here. I can tell."

"And you? Would you like me here?"

She straightened her back slightly, gave me a strict, matronly look, folding her arms before her, closing off. "I don't care. I really don't." She muttered something I could not make out and left me to the books and my thoughts.

It made sense for me to move to Winter Willow. I knew that. I wouldn't have to pay rent, Stone had said as much. It was even closer to the university, but I worried moving there would mean I'd lose much more than my privacy. Since coming to Winter Willow most days for a week, I had come to sense a somnolence to the house, something that left me sleepy and unable to react or think clearly. As I was pondering why this was, I heard Stone behind me. "What are you doing with those books?" he asked. I had not spoken to him since our conversation a few days before when he left annoyed and I did not want to provoke him further.

"I thought I'd sort alphabetically and put them in the shelves here," I said pointing to the large bookcase behind his desk, to the right of the window.

"Without checking with me?" He straightened, which gave the impression that he was rearing up irritably before me. "I've reserved that bookcase for my work, for the translations and critical studies. I told you this when you came here."

He had not, or at least I did not recall him telling me this. "I didn't realize," I said.

Before I could say more, he said, "No, you don't realize. You can't realize. You don't even realize who I am, how important I've been." He was right. I knew little about his work, had only a vague recollection of the characters or plot of the book he was most famous for. Even though his novel was still on the curriculum for many high schools, I knew his popularity had fallen, that to many scholars his work was considered a novelty, its import merely an artifact from the past. I thought how I should read his work again. It might help explain him, I reasoned, and whether he had been mistreated or misunderstood by modern readers and critics, as his chagrin implied.

"Those idiots working today," he muttered turning from me. I wasn't sure whom he was referring to but knew better than to ask. "I was feted everywhere. And you'll see, when I release my new book, you'll see."

"So you're writing?"

"Yes, of course. I've never stopped." He looked back to me. *Spitting mad* was a term my mother had used to describe when a person became so angry they seemed defined solely by their anger, and I thought as I looked at him that these words fit him perfectly.

I knew enough to remain silent and went back to the bookcase, removing books, twisting my head to read their titles, trying to ignore his seething presence. "Good," he said, when he saw me stacking the books and dusting the shelves.

Like Celeste, he seemed to know about my housing dilemma and took it as fact I would be moving in with them. When I was dressing to leave he came to the top of the staircase of the second floor and looked down at me, "I'm expecting you'll move in next weekend," he said, then disappeared back to his study.

. . .

After having spent the morning at Winter Willow, that afternoon when I went to the library at the university, I found I was again unable to concentrate. I was to meet with Professor Edison in a few days and I'd not thought about what I would say to her. I knew I needed to concentrate, set goals, read, think, but it seemed my ambition was falling away from me, and I was having difficulty caring about my thesis and degree.

What kind of weariness was this? Soul heaviness, I thought, brought on by all the turns that had left me on that January afternoon feeling alone in the large reading room, with its students bent in earnest study and its row upon row of books. Out the window I could see people below on the windy pathways, dressed in bulky coats, walking as quickly as they could to escape the bitterness of the day. This parade of students interested me far more than the book before me. I was hungry, closed the journal, put my pen and notebook back in my satchel and left for the food court in a nearby building. There I ordered a sandwich to take back to my room. This was not my usual routine. In the past, I'd often spend all day and most of the night reading in the library, but on this day I felt a certain claustrophobia sitting at the desk, other students close by, all locked in their concentrated pursuits. I realized that that sort of focus was beyond me at that moment and watching them made me aware that I needed to find a place where I could be alone and think about where fate was leading me.

. . .

Back at the rooming house, before I took off my boots and coat, I stood for a moment with my back to the door and looked at the space before me, at the fierce winter sun moving slowly over the objects there, the mess of books around the bed, on the chairs and shelves. The curtains moved in the soft current of air from the heat register that filled the room with dry warmth. At that moment, I decided I'd move to Winter Willow. It made sense on many levels and I was hoping it would provide a safe harbour for me to once again find meaning in my studies, a meaning that had been so important and had sustained me in the past.

Other than my books, I possessed few personal items—clothes, a portable typewriter, toiletries, makeup—things easy enough to move. And my mother's chair which sat in the middle of the room. It sat like my mother herself, a central object in my life, and I had to admit when I was thinking of the logistics of my move, an encumbrance. The thought made me sad, until I remembered Elsa had always loved the chair, would sit in it and play with the levers when she'd come over for tea or talk. And so at that moment I decided I would give it to her, and my mood lightened as I took off my boots and flung my coat on the back of that chair.

. . .

When I told Elsa she could have the chair which had been my mother's, she said, "No, I won't keep it. When you want it back, it will be here." She was sitting at the small table, drinking the cup of tea I'd made for her. Her hair was pulled into a high ponytail and frizzy grey strands had broken free around her face.

"I don't know, Elsa, when I'll have a place where I can use it."

"Well when you do, you can have it back." In a few weeks she was to relocate to the second floor, as Eve had decided to move. After telling me of her plans she said, "Which reminds me, Eve told me to tell you that her boyfriend has a van and he can move you when you want."

I was relieved to think I had the problem of the move resolved. "I've decided I'll go to Winter Willow next Friday. It's not far, you know on that street with the old mansions."

"Yes, I do know the street, but do you think it's a good idea?"

"Probably not, but it's expeditious."

"I'd be careful," she said, looking away from me. I had called her from the hallway before she'd had a chance to enter her own room and snow from her boots was melting beneath her chair. I noticed the long green scarf she'd wound around her neck was resting in the puddle.

"Oh, Elsa, your scarf," I said, rescuing it.

"You won't forget me, will you Melanie?" she asked as I, closer now, draped the scarf on the table.

"Of course not. I'll come back to visit. I promise."

Her large hand patted mine. "Good, that's good," she said.

◆ ◆ ◆

After Elsa left and I sat down in the chair I'd promised her, it was with a sense that things were falling into place, and the thought crossed my mind that Winter Willow—its rooms and brooding silences—seemed to have been waiting for me all the years I'd walked before its broad façade on my way to or from the university.

◆ ◆ ◆

Shortly after I arrived at Winter Willow the next morning, the doorbell echoed, a solemn sound that rang through the rooms like a premonition. I heard Celeste open the door and say, "Oh Gavin, how good to see you." And after a moment's pause. "Here, let me take your coat." When I came to the door of the library Celeste said, "This is Melanie. She's helping with organizing Stone's library." He offered his hand, which I shook. "Melanie, this is Gavin, Stone's solicitor." He had a full grey moustache and despite the fact that he must have been at least in his late sixties, his hair was a thick and disheveled mass when he took off his hat, a furred object with side flaps that made his head look huge. A large man, his bulk seemed to fill the space in the foyer between Celeste and me, and despite his age, the slightly bulging eyes beneath the frowning brow were lively and piqued with the mischief of a much younger man.

"And friend," he added without letting his gaze leave me. "So you're the student working with Stone. Well isn't he the crafty one."

"What do you mean?" I said, but before he could answer, Celeste interrupted.

"Stone is upstairs. I know he's awake so he's probably in the library."

After he'd left, Celeste said, "He's a writer too, or was years ago. Gavin Sheldon? Have you heard of him?"

"No, doesn't ring a bell."

She looked at me closely and then critically. The days I'd been there, after she let me in in the early morning, we'd barely seen each other. She stayed in the kitchen but twice when I was there at lunch-time, she came to the room where I was working to ask if I wanted to have lunch with her. And when I said yes, we ate together at the small table in the middle of the room that looked out to the garden. An excellent, if unadventurous cook, she made soup and either a salad or sandwich for our lunches.

On the day of Gavin's visit, as we sat eating together, I asked how she ended up at Winter Willow. "I used to write poetry," she said and when I looked at her with a questioning expression, she continued. "That meant I went to readings and the like."

"Do you still? Write, I mean."

"Oh no. I was not that good. But it allowed me to meet Stone at one of the literary events." She bent further over her soup, avoiding my eyes, as I knew she was trying to avoid my questions. And I had questions. By my reckoning she was at least twenty years younger than Stone, in her sixties. And if she had met him when she was in her thirties, that would have been when Stone was married to his second wife. I knew this because I had tracked down a *Who's Who* in the library, which gave a chronology of his life. I wondered when Celeste had become part of that chronology, when she started living at Winter Willow. But my real question was, what did it give her to spend her life there, in those quiet rooms? She could sense my curiosity and quickly stood, gathering plates and clearing the table in order to avoid being confronted by my questions.

# 7

When I moved to Winter Willow the following Friday, I left behind the jovial activity and bantering of Eve and her friends. After dragging my chair to Elsa's room across the hall, we packed the van with my suitcases, boxes, clothes, and other items, depositing them in my room at Winter Willow. Alone there, surrounded by my belongings, I was struck by the deadening quiet of my new home. After she'd opened the door to me, I did not see Celeste again that night. Nor did I see Stone, who did not leave his room to greet me. I sat on the floor and felt desolate in that large, high-ceiling space. My room, like all the rooms of Stone's house that I'd seen, had wide chair and ceiling mouldings and high baseboards; its curtains were heavy brocade in a silvery blue pattern of birds and flowers. Furniture—the bed's headboard and two matching chairs—were upholstered in the same muted fabric. I lay on the bedspread, pulled a blanket from the foot of the mattress, and longed for the room I'd just left behind—that space now lost to me forever.

Later I left Winter Willow and walked toward the university, where I found a takeout restaurant. I brought a sandwich and salad back to my room as the sun was setting, and the day became darker and colder. When I entered the house, all the rooms I could see on the ground floor were dark and there was a dim light past the staircase coming from, I assumed, the suite of rooms where Celeste stayed. A dull light lit the second floor, and when I passed Stone's room I saw that his light was on. I noted that the hallway was now heated and I was grateful that decision had been made. Past my room, at the end of the hall, was the door that led to the third floor. I stopped and looked at it, my hand on the doorknob of my room. I was curious what I'd find there. From the street, I'd noted there were four peaked dormer windows with closed grey shutters.

Before entering my room, I walked soundlessly to the end of the hall and tested the door leading to the third floor. It was locked. I twisted it again. Definitely locked. I wondered if it had always been or if the lock was new and meant solely for me.

. . .

The next morning when I heard a knock and opened the door, Stone was before me holding a box, which I could see contained a blue silk dress with sapphire beads. He extended it toward me. "For you," he said. I lifted the dress free from the box and held it against myself.

"Oh, my mother would have loved this," I said, as Stone stood admiring the dress, shifting his head from side to side. "But I really can't accept it."

"Of course you can."

I looked down at the fringe of blue beads sown to the bodice, the silk sash which caught the light and shone silver-blue.

"I bought it in London, after the war," Stone said as he watched me appraising the garment.

"It's lovely." I let the dress drop away from me. Stone would know what it meant that the gift he offered was from London in the 1920s, and he'd know too how much it would please me. I felt awkward and suddenly shy taking the dress but also a little honoured for it had been a long time since anyone had given me a gift.

"It was hers, but she sent it back to me."

"Hers?"

"Yes, I bought it for my first wife, Catherine."

With it weighted in my hands, I thought what it had meant all those years ago and wondered where she had worn it. Perhaps she walked on the heath between Hampstead and High Gate while the woods grew weary with night and the gems of her dress would have shone like blue stars.

"She must have loved it. And I'm sure it made her very proud to wear it."

"It was an unusual time and not a particularly happy one, I'd say. I started my novel then." As he spoke, he backed away from me into the hallway. I knew he was abandoning our conversation, and I wondered if it was his wife he did not want to speak about, or the war.

"We should discuss this sometime—your impression." He looked at me but remained quiet. His face was drawn, and I recognized sadness in its expression, in the droop of the skin around his eyes.

He turned away. "You don't need to take it if you don't like it," he said, his gaze leaving me, looking down the hallway to the staircase.

"But I love it."

He came back then, leaned toward me so close I could see the pale blue watery colour of his eyes. "It was a difficult time. I've been thinking of it lately but I'm sure it's nothing like how you imagine it." He took the dress from my hands and placed it back in the box. "And I was young. Things are always viewed differently when you're young. It's only many years later when you recall the time, that things fit into a whole life, when they find their true significance."

He left me then in the doorway and as I watched him leave, enter his room, I clenched the box against my chest.

In my room, I placed the dress on one of the hangers in the closet. I was about to discard the box when I saw the shape of an envelope through the tissue the dress had been wrapped in.

It was a yellowed envelope addressed to Stone at Winter Willow, and I knew it had been read because the envelope was ripped open. Inside was a single sheet, folded with neat handwriting in black ink:

*My dear Stone,*

*These words come to me as I pack this dress in tissue and fold it into the box, words I know you will appreciate:* Rich gifts wax poor when givers prove unkind. *And yet I know it was something much larger than you or what happened to us that was unkind. It was a certain fate from our era. How naïve I was to think it would not touch us, that we could escape, and life would continue as it had before you went to war.*

*When I see this dress, something breaks inside me. It had seemed all those years ago to represent something like a promise, and I guess there's no other way to think of it now, but as a promise broken. I could not abide keeping it, and yet I could not either discard it. And so I am sending it back to you.*

I turned the sheet over to continue reading.

*This is difficult to write, but I feel it best to stop all correspondence, not that you've attempted to contact me, I realize. Your mother has, of course, with details of the divorce but there has been nothing from you. And now, almost a year since you left with your mother, left me alone here, I believe it is time for me to move on. And I will, but you must know that I do so with something of your sweetness, your kindness and, yes, your cruelty lodged in me, lodged very close to my heart. And so, in weariness, I close this chapter (to couch this in a metaphor you'd understand) to begin another, away from you and your memory.*

*Catherine*

I sat on the edge of the bed, the letter loose in my hand, and stared at the space before me. What is this place where I have decided to live, I wondered. What stories hidden here? The letter seemed to imply that the dress was bought either before or during the war. Was he confused when he told me it was after the war or did he want

me to value the garment as coming from that era that most fascinated me? A sense of uncertainty piqued with trepidation settled in
me, as formidable as the silence that filled every room in that grand
old house.

. . .

After Stone's visit to my room and reading Catherine's letter, I ate
breakfast in the dull-lit kitchen and watched the beginning of a snowstorm in the silent garden. And with the snow a slowness seemed to
move in, not only there but in all the rooms of that house—rooms
where Celeste, Stone and I stayed in our separate spaces. That day,
Celeste told me if I wanted, I could join her for dinner in the kitchen.
Stone, she said, usually took his meals in his room. During the day I'd
be in the downstairs library, Stone in the library upstairs and Celeste
in the kitchen at the back of the house, or so I assumed as I would not
see or hear either of them for hours. For a week the days followed this
simple routine, a week when I did not go to the university. I had left
a message for my advisor saying I was ill, which was not exactly true,
unless the malaise of winter could be considered an illness.

At night after dinner, leaving Celeste in the kitchen, I would
retire to my room to read. There were no televisions in the house,
which suited me, but I found the silence—a silence I'd drop my book
at times to listen to—isolating. At other times the house seemed to
moan as if burdened by the weight of snow or the assault of wind.
The floors creaked when I walked on them, and often there was a
whistling sound as the wind became trapped in a window or door.
In the middle of the night, on occasion, I thought I could hear noise
coming from the rooms above me, from the third floor. It would be
in the deadest hours when I normally would be asleep and once I
woke and was sure I heard the high pitch squeal of a door opening
or closing. Could Stone or Celeste be visiting the third floor, I wondered? But then sleep overtook me and my suspicions.

I moved through those days as if partially asleep and had

difficulty resisting the urge to close my eyes as I cataloged the seemingly endless books of Stone's library. Snow gathered, piled on the front porch, ladened the back garden, balanced on the sills of windows, the door thresholds. "Isn't it pretty?" Celeste said one morning when I went to the kitchen to make toast. Her look of calm happiness, the slight smile, were unexpected and in contrast to the usual glumness with which she greeted me and the day.

"Yes," I said, simply. She was in an unusually talkative mood.

"These days are hard on Stone."

"These days?"

"I mean housebound in this weather. He's a writer; he knows melancholy."

The toast popped and I placed it on my plate and went to sit by her at the table. "Who doesn't feel that way this time of year?"

"You're so young," she said.

This was the second time she had shut me down with this statement and I felt a fresh irritation. "Not so young that I don't know melancholy or loss," I said.

"You could never understand him, that's all I mean." She left the room, and while I ate alone at the table, I thought how little desire I had to understand him. When she returned a few moments later, she continued. "He's had so much loss, two wives died, another left without explanation." I knew the outline of his life from reading his entry in *Who's Who*, but I thought at that moment that there must be biographies or articles in the stacks I could read, and I made a vow to do that when I returned to my routine at the library. I thought then how I missed the calm of that space—looking up to see the reading room widen away from me, the silent movement of people entering and leaving, their ballet of silence that corresponded somehow to an internal movement of contemplation.

Before leaving the kitchen, she stopped and turned to me. "Why are you not nicer to him?" she said. She was standing by the doorway and her stare surprised me with its intensity.

"Really? Lately I barely see him." And when I do, I thought, his tone is usually gruff with me. Since the day he made it clear he did not wish to speak of his time in London and later when he gave me the gown, his tone had been dismissive. I did not see him as a man who enjoyed my company, but I was not about to discuss any of this with Celeste.

· · ·

On the afternoon of the following Monday, Stone came to the door of the library where I was working, "I want you to start organizing my letters, those I received from my publisher and readers. They need to be put in order for the archives."

"All right. Do you want me to start that before I finish sorting through the books?"

"Before. They're upstairs."

Lately I'd been sleeping longer in the morning and beginning my work in Stone's library in the afternoons. I knew, because Celeste mentioned it, that food was delivered weekly, the same type of food, every week, because "he likes routine". She also told me that once a week a charwoman came in, but I had yet to see her. Other than these simple intrusions, and on occasion Gavin, Stone's solicitor, no one visited. The whole busy frantic world slipped by outside the gates of Winter Willow—as I had slipped by it for years—with only a fleeting glance toward the house with its ordered rooms and monastic silence.

Here is a truth I've discovered: patterns assert themselves in a life, until there is a series of patterns, which itself becomes a pattern. When I lived in the rooming house and heard about the withdrawal of my funding, that routine, with all its incumbent solace, ended when the writing program was cancelled. And now, during the remaining weeks of January at Winter Willow another routine was being established. I look back on those weeks, at the way the days were often made sleepy by falling snow I could see through windows, blowing in the yard or on the street, and see in it a comfort that came to mark the time. I spent hours in either the downstairs library in its failing light or the second-floor library, where there was desk for my sorting and categorizing of Stone's letters and correspondence. I quickly fell into a routine of reading at night in my room, and when I heard the haunted sound of wind as it circled the house, I would be consoled by the warmth of the quilt I pulled over me. Could it only be three weeks since I moved in and a little over a month since I met Stone? I wondered one morning alone in my bed. But just as the full paralysis of winter struck, so did change of a different sort.

# 8

One morning a month after my move to Winter Willow, when one of the many snowstorms of the year had stopped, the sun came out brilliant and blinding on the abundant white of the back garden. It alighted on roofs, fences, streetlamps with a crystalline intensity. While I was working in the first-floor library, lit by the strong, sterile light that stretched into the room from the large front window, Stone came to the door.

"I'm going to hold a party, invite some of the people I used to know from my university years," he said, his voice calm but with a rare congeniality to it.

"Do you want me to organize it?" I said.

"No, it will be a simple affair with caterers and such. I just want to make sure you will be available to attend."

"If you want me to, I will."

"And I want you to wear that dress I gave you, the one you said your mother would like." What did it matter to him what I wore? Was I to represent something to the people he would invite? An acquisition, perhaps?

Contemplating his motives left me uncertain of how to deal with his request, and a little confused, so I changed the topic. "I'm on my way to the university. I need to see my advisor."

"Go," he said, lifting his arm as if to shoo me away, after which he turned and left the room.

• • •

My academic supervisor, Professor Edison, lacked the kind of social grace that allowed pleasantries and often displayed, at least when dealing with me, a distracted boredom. I knew she would have preferred to not have me as a student, but on this day when I came into her office, she smiled and said, without preamble, "I hear you're living with Stone Shackelford."

"I'm living there because I'm working for him, and my rooming house had been sold." Then I said defensively, "how did you hear that?"

"Someone here, a professor emeritus who knows him, he told me."

"Really? What did he say?"

"Well, Shackelford's obviously told his friends. And I believe there's to be a gathering with some of these old buddies and other people from the faculty." She turned her head to look at me as if her right eye was better able to discern the truth. And what was the truth? If Stone had been telling his friends about me, I wondered if it was in any way couched in innuendo. And I wondered why I was only hearing about the party now, when other people had already been invited.

"Really? People are talking about this? You know how old he is, don't you?"

"Well, yes, of course." Her tone became sharp. "And I didn't mean to imply anything."

"Then why are we talking about this?" She was surprised by my harsh response; I could see that. Her eyes narrowed, and she leaned back in the chair, watching me. "The idea is absurd," I said. "He's not, well it's not like that."

She gave a low, non-committal hum, came forward in the chair, and we went on to speak about my recent readings. It was difficult to follow her or explain what I had read as I kept thinking of Stone and wondering what he'd been saying to people, or what he had left unsaid. At the end of the session Professor Edison said I needed to speed up my reading and start working on the thesis. "I know you've been ill, and I guess the disruption of the move made it difficult to concentrate, but you need to hasten this thesis." She was quiet for a moment, which made me turn from my thoughts of Stone to look at her. And when I did, I saw her concentration had drifted from me, and her expression seemed one of worry. Her attention snapped back when she saw me looking at her so closely. "And next time I want to see at least some preliminary notes toward the structure of the manuscript."

. . .

Walking back to Winter Willow my thoughts stalled on the role I played in Stone's life. It brought to mind that once, when kneeling on the floor shifting through books I'd put there for easier sorting, I glanced up to see him looking down at me. He seemed in a trance, his look of blank withdrawal so unnerving that I said, "Stone," gently. He shook the look off and made a grunt before going back to his book.

When I arrived, I entered by the front door, the only door I had a key for, and Celeste came from the back room, wiping her hands on a dish towel. "Still cold?" she said.

"Where is Stone?" I ignored her question. "I need to speak with him."

She knew by the way I was rushed, distracted, that I was upset. "Upstairs, I think, but don't bother him. He's working." I moved around her to climb the steps. I had not removed my boots or coat but had opened the wool scarf around my neck. He was in the library, on the settee, and he put the book he was reading down when I entered the room.

"Stone," I said. "I'm hearing things at the university."

"Like what?" he said.

"I'm not even sure, but people are talking about us and I find it upsetting."

"People talk. They always talk."

"Well I don't like it," I said. "And the implication is not true."

"Melanie, this is what happens. It means nothing."

"But it does mean something."

"And what is that?" With an effort, he gripped the arm of the settee to stand and came toward me.

"I'm not sure, but it makes me angry," I said and moved away from him, but he reached me and held me by my forearms, the first time he touched me.

"You know Melanie," he said in a softened voice. I could see the sore wateriness of his eyes, their pink rim, their sad look, and I jerked my arms from his grasp. "I've lived a long time and I've learnt that we all have secrets and these secrets are never the things that people guess or speak about." I tugged away from him. "The most important thing you will learn, my dear, during this time in your life, is what to ignore."

I saw an earnestness in his expression that surprised me. I rubbed the back of my arm, moved to the door, and opening it said, "I'm not sure what you mean, but I do know that I moved here to work, not be part of your life." He was turned from me, so I could not see his reaction, but I saw him stop and his back stiffen, and I knew he'd heard me. When he turned, his face was blotched. It frightened me how ill he looked, and I realized then that he was not well, that he was faltering.

"You are the most ungrateful girl."

"No..." Looking at him, seeing the grey tone of his face, I couldn't finish my thought and I let the sentence drop.

"Get out," he said with determination. When I did not move, wondering if I should offer to get him something—water, medication, to help him lie down perhaps, he said louder with unmasked irritation, "I said, get out."

In the hallway, Celeste hissed, "I told you. I told you not to upset him." I did not answer. Instead I descended the stairs, stopped for a moment in the silence of the main hall before opening the door. The afternoon sky was clear blue and the street, with its mounds of snow in the yards and on the roofs of houses, had the quality of a precise etching, as if the snowfall had clarified and cleansed the air. I busied myself against the cold, walking with purpose once again to the university.

. . .

In the library, I found a remote corner with a single desk, dumped my coat, hat, scarf and went to the stacks to look for a book of stories by Katherine Mansfield. She would steady me, I thought. I settled on the story, *The Daughters of the Late Colonel*, and soon I felt like I was withdrawing from my current concerns, placing them in context of a larger truth, transported by the sister's conversation, the situation of their life after the death of their father. As I was finishing the story, someone touched my shoulder.

"Hey," he whispered. Martin Mackenzie. The student I'd met in the office of my supervisor. "I'm glad I ran into you. Can you spare a few minutes?"

I gathered my satchel and we went to the lounge on the main floor where we could speak. "I love this place," he said settling into one of the large, wooden-framed chairs. It was a simple statement, something I also had often felt and hearing him say it made me feel immediately at ease with him.

"Me too," I said. "Always feel so at home here."

"So, I've been looking for you. There's been some trouble with Helen." I knew my supervisor's first name was Helen, but I had never heard anyone use it before.

"What sort of trouble?"

"A plagiarism accusation. A student she had a few years ago says Helen stole her thesis."

"Really? That doesn't sound like her."

"I don't know all the details," he said. "And administration is keeping the facts closely guarded. But they are investigating and in the meantime, her grad students are being distributed to other profs."

He looked down, then lifted his eyes so that I could see their clear blueness. "Did she say anything to you? I mean when you last met?"

"Are you kidding? She never speaks with me about her personal life; thinks my thesis is useless too." Martin smiled at what I said, or was it the beginning of a laugh? He had a way of saying something clever and quickly looking away, as if what he'd expressed was a prank from which he had to distance himself. It made him seem distracted, as if he was able to see the comical undertone in every situation. I came to find his attitude disarming, but later, when I knew him better, he told me it was actually fear and nervousness that made him jumpy and eager to amuse.

He was dressed in worn jeans, heavy construction boots in the same caramel colour that Elsa's had been. "I saw you the first day I came here," he said. "I saw you but I'm sure you didn't notice me."

"And when was that?" I said. "When did you come here?"

"Over a month ago—for the winter term. I know it's weird to come halfway through the year, but I needed a change."

"And you saw me here? In the library?"

"No, in your office in the English department. But you were so intent on reading your book you didn't notice me." We were sitting kitty corner to each other, and with this statement and not being able to think what to say next, we sat quiet, occasionally looking forward and scanning the room. At one point when he and I glanced up at the same instant, I felt an intensifying of interest. I wanted to know what he thought, to see his crooked smile and to laugh with him. How quickly I fell into this view of him. Years later, I would look back on that afternoon and evening and see in the day the pivot upon which so much changed—and it all happened so quietly and irreversibly, even though it took me a while to know or acknowledge the difference made by that calm, funny, and serious meeting in the library lounge.

# 9

I'd had a boyfriend for almost two years in high school, long enough to fall into a pattern of mutual dependence. Tall, bushy-haired with a dark manliness about him, thick-limbed, he was someone who could have easily been an athlete. But he had no desire to be part of these activities; instead he decided he wanted to be a writer.

One Sunday night a few months before I was to leave for university, Joni came across the hall and asked my mother if she could speak with me. My mother, without comment, brought her to my room, where I was reading on the bed. Joni and I did not see each other as much as we had in the past, mostly because her boyfriend lived in the country and she'd spend her weekends with him. I was surprised to see her, and once the door was closed, before I could say anything, she said, "God. This is hard to say."

"What? What is it?" I was worried something had happened to her family, for it had always seemed a possibility to me that her sister or one of her brothers would meet with a calamity of some sort.

"I saw your boyfriend last night at the fair with another girl."

"But he told me he was visiting his brother. Are you sure?"

"Yeah. I'm sure. He didn't see me, so I followed them for a bit, and I'm sure it was him." The shock of hearing this was like a sudden cold waterfall flowing over me.

Joni crossed the room to sit close beside me on the bed. "He doesn't deserve you, you know." She draped her arm across my shoulder as I sat stiffly, not sure what I was feeling, beyond shock.

• ◆ •

A few days later, after first saying it was not true, but then admitting it was, he said he'd decided he wanted to begin his university life unencumbered—that was the word he used. I moved two months later to the city where I began my own undergraduate work, but this turn of events had created a pall over my first months away from home. I lived in the dorm surrounded by girls, all of whom were loud and exuberant and foolish as rabbits set free. By comparison, I was quiet, with feelings so sensitive that these girls learnt to keep their distance.

◆ • ◆

Two years before I met Stone and moved to Winter Willow, I'd had an affair with a visiting scholar, an affair no one in the department knew about. He was an expert on Nabokov and when our liaison began I thought we could be together as a couple, even though he was more than twenty years older than I was. He gave me a key to his apartment and I'd often go there, and we'd make dinner, drink wine, and spend the rest of the evening in bed. I struggle to remember this liaison now—the feel of his hand moving over my body, I do remember that, and the tangling of my legs around his, as I struggled to rise above him, showing my long, young body to him. I knew by his expression that he was always touched when I did this, he would open his mouth as if to say something but instead his eyes would glisten and rather than speak, he'd pull me down to him. Our lovemaking was vigorous and always left me with the desire to laugh, to hold him while I laughed. It was with him that I learnt the value of lovemaking in a relationship—the freedom it gave, and its ability to link people, but also a sense of abandonment that was deeply personal.

I brought him to meet my mother, who asked that he sleep in the living room and not share my childhood room with me. At the time I thought she was reacting in a way she thought a responsible, or conventionally moral, parent would react. But later she told me she did not feel comfortable with him in the apartment, that she sensed there was something about him that was untrustworthy. "I mean look at him, he's probably old enough to be your father." If that were true, it made him old enough to be her husband, but I stayed away from that thought and said nothing in response.

One day in the library after a weekend of not being able to get in touch with him, I saw him in the quad outside the window, speaking to a woman. He was laughing, running his hand through his thick, unruly mass of dark hair, looking away and then looking back at this woman who, like me, was tall and blonde, and who stood smiling discretely as if she recognized his performance for the sham it was. Watching them, I thought how it could have been me down there listening to him just a few months earlier and I wondered if he was using some of the same language he'd used with me. I knew in that instant, regardless of what the issues between him and this woman were, that our relationship was near its end, that we were now going to, and were meant to, drift apart. What surprised me was that I was not more hurt by the end of our affair, that I felt, in the final analysis, it was merely how it was meant to unfold.

Two months later he accepted a position at a university on the west coast, and a few years after that I heard he became engaged to a student with whom he quickly had two children. I thought of this gratefully as the fate I had avoided.

. . .

"What's your thesis on?" Martin asked.

"The '20s, Woolf, Eliot, after the war."

"Interesting time. Mine's on the Montreal poets, Klein, Smith, Page, that gang."

Over the years, I've tried to define what happened that day in the lounge of the library—the joy and confusion of Martin and our first meeting. To an observer, it was a simple, even common, scene of students speaking, enjoying themselves certainly, but there would have been no indication of what was beginning to stir and hold us together.

Visiting the south of France, years later, I went to a gallery which had been the house of the artist Marc Chagall, and when I saw his work, its vibrant colour, the ephemeral lightness of his images, I felt it was the closest representation to the feelings awakened that day in the library with Martin.

We stayed in the lounge for an hour, until the evening settled black against the window at the far end of the room, mirroring us in its dark plane. He was in turn funny, serious, concerned about me, kind, considerate and teasing. And I was to remember the things he said, the words like smooth stones in my pocket, words which my mind could recall, which brought back the lightness of our conversation and of our being together.

After two hours in the lounge, Martin said, "Let's go for dinner somewhere". I had only a few dollars, so suggested the university food court. I knew Celeste would be waiting for me, that she'd have made enough food for three and be angry when I didn't return home, but I did not want to be in that house with its secret grievances and regrets and I did, more than anything, want to stay with Martin.

The temperature had lifted and when we left the library it was not necessary to use our scarves or gloves, and this too added to the sense of freedom, of opening up to a time not confined by the heavy enclosure of winter. As we were eating—a hamburger for Martin, salad for me—I said, "Have you heard of Stone Shackelford?"

"The writer? Yeah. He lives close to here, doesn't he? A recluse, I heard."

"Well, I work for him."

"Really?" He frowned. "Doing what?"

"Arranging his library, correspondence, stuff like that. I started after I lost my funding."

"Helen did that to you, you know. I heard her on the phone." He scrunched the paper that had covered his hamburger and pitched it in the garbage bin behind me. "She's jealous."

I told Martin then of my first meeting with Stone when he made a statement about attractiveness not always being the gift it appears. I told him too about how I'd entered the back garden and been surprised by Stone, and how that led to my position, but as I spoke, I noticed he was fidgeting, that he'd sat back in his chair, and was looking away from me. I stopped. "What are you thinking about?" I said.

"How I knew I'd like you."

"Really?"

"How I knew it'd be difficult though." He looked down at his hands folded on the table.

"What? Liking me?" I smiled. He glanced at me but quickly looked away.

"No, just everything, as you get older, it's more difficult." For the first time since we had sat together, I felt removed from him and I had no idea what he was thinking.

"I'm not so sure about that," I said. "It's easy right now. Sitting here, the weather letting up a bit, allowing us to think they'll be a time out of the deep freeze. Actually, it's the opposite of difficult tonight." And I meant it. Since I'd moved to Winter Willow, I felt as if I were submerged in a cold place where I was unable to move or think clearly, captive under the heavy permanence of a winter storm, a time when I'd lost the will to take charge of my future.

"Well, that's a hopeful attitude," he said, a smile brightening his face.

◆ ◆ ◆

On the sidewalk after I left Martin, I wrapped the scarf around my throat to guard against the wind which had picked up since we went to eat. I realized I was smiling and there was a gaiety to my thoughts that allowed me to feel an unfamiliar happiness. Being with Martin had given me a sense that there were options for my life which I'd been ignoring. In this state of mind, I thought of my mother, but not of her death, rather the way she had been when we lived together. I thought how the rooms of our apartment would be now occupied by another family and how there was only me left who remembered our lives there from so long ago.

The night was lit by a full moon's stark whiteness, and when I stood on the pathway leading to the back door of Stone's house, the same pathway which had led to the garden I'd followed on the first day I went there, I was reluctant to enter Winter Willow. I thought of Stone, how he'd given me a home, a salary, something to do. I knew that the view he had of his achievements and importance was so clear to him that his grandiosity could fill the rooms of that large house, even when he railed against a world that had passed him by. Yet as a young man, he'd learnt how the spirit could be broken by war and the heartbreak of losing someone dear to him as a result. Surely this wounded young man's evolution into this delusional old man was only possible through years of something like regret, years of living with a mother, with two wives, and finally with Celeste that allowed his world to shrink to the rooms of Winter Willow. In studying life after the First World War, I felt I'd be able to not only grasp the era that produced the literature I loved, but now also to learn who Stone was and why he became the person he became.

He must know, I reasoned, in the deep, unquestioning part of his mind where there is access to truth, that his influence and import-ance was now a thing of the past. Standing on the path, I looked up at the lit windows of Stone's room and admitted I could not know what that falling into redundancy would feel like. I'd witnessed Stone's need to delude, to willfully ignore what was clear to everyone else, and I thought how necessary these strategies were for his sense of self. In the past weeks, I'd learnt these things about Stone. What I didn't know, hesitating before entering that grand house, unsure where my life was to take me, was how our relationship was to change.

# 10

"There you are," Celeste said. "I waited for you."

"Well, you shouldn't have. I met a friend."

"You've upset him." She had opened the door to me and after I passed through the veranda and entered the room made hot by the oven, she stood in the middle of the kitchen, exuding a combative energy. I moved around her to reach the hallway where I hung up my coat in the closet, and she followed. "He was upset by what you said, and then when you did not come back, well, he became more upset."

"I don't think I have that kind of impact on him, Celeste." My voice was bitter and harsh, and I hoped it would stop her talking so that I could find the way to my room where I could be alone.

"Well, he was smashing things upstairs. I heard him, before dinner." Anxiety radiated from her like heat. "Please. Go see him."

"No, I'm tired. I only want to sleep."

"I heard him call your name, when the door opened. Go to him. That's the least you can do."

When I reached the second floor and saw the light under his door, I knocked. He said to enter and when I did, he was propped up on the bed, pillows behind him, his arm across his face in a pose I found dramatic and strangely feminine. Then I saw blood on the bedding and realized it was his.

He had somehow managed to break the glass on a bookcase and had either stood or walked through the shards, cutting his foot. I had never seen his feet before and seeing them now surprised me—the translucent flesh over the slender bones, delicate and ordered under the skin, like fish submerged in icy water. "Oh God, Stone, what have you done?"

"Leave me alone, just leave." He moved his arm so that I could see blank sadness in his face, blood on the cuff of the arm of his pajama top and the gaze that would not move from the space directly before him.

"I'm sorry, Stone, if I upset you." And seeing him in such a state, I was sorry.

He moved his arm back over his eyes.

"I said what I said as a way to hurt." He lifted his arm then and looked directly at me. "It makes me angry though that people would think you're taking advantage of me like that."

"Or, you're taking advantage of me," he said, letting his arm fall beside him. I came to the side of the bed and he sat up, reached for my waist, and leaned his head against my hip. At this moment I could have pushed him away. But this was the person I was then, full of my own needs I suppose, fearful of offending, because I did not push him away. "I'm cancelling the soiree. It upset you too much," he said before letting me go. As I turned to leave, he said, "I've been thinking, Melanie."

"Yes." I faced him.

"I've been thinking about your interest in London, after the war, how it affected life then. You've made me think of it."

"Was that a cruel thing to do?" I asked.

"No, but you're right. I don't like to speak of it, it brings me back there and it took years to forget." His gaze shifted from me to the corner of the room. "But then you never really do forget. It was the constant thought of dying, knowing it could come at any moment, that it had come for others, young men who were your friends or compatriots. Having seen it, in fact."

He sighed, faced the window and appeared so withdrawn that one would have thought he was alone. The sheer curtains that fell to the floor waved in the weak ooze of the radiator's heat, the only movement in the room.

"I had a friend, someone from here, from Canada, we attended the same university, and we went together to the war. One day after a game of poker which he'd won, when he was walking away, gloating, making a joke, something he'd done many times, there was an explosion, a mortar shell, and he was gone. Just gone." I knew that in Stone's recollection at that moment, he was alone, that the memory was so traumatic that it had created a gulf I could not traverse, even with my desire to know more.

I stood silent, watching him. The moments moved on. His gaze did not waver, and it seemed as his voice filled with emotion that his eyes filled as well with sorrow. "Like you, she never understood."

"What?" I said.

"Catherine. She couldn't understand how it made me feel. Why, when I was home safely with her, with the war over, I could still know such fear."

"So what happened?"

"What always happens. We lost each other." He glanced down, picked up a piece of paper idly, part of a stack that was on the bed. "You know the way people say they lost touch, it's a common enough saying, but that's what happened—we lost touch, something intimate was gone."

He wanted to talk I could tell. In the aftermath of the trauma between us, he was now calm, as if after surviving a treacherous storm he'd found silence and comfort in its aftermath. "Is that when you came home?" I said. I'd opened the door to leave and was leaning on the door jamb.

"My mother came over to London. I'd been ill and she brought me home."

"And your wife, Catherine?"

"She stayed." When he looked at me something hardened in his expression. I could see his realization that he was sharing more than he meant. "I think that's enough reminiscing for today." He rose from the bed slowly. "I'll say goodnight, Melanie."

"Stone," I said, and he turned back to me. "Stone, I've been thinking, we should not let other people stop us from having the party if you really want it. It doesn't seem right."

He did not answer but tilted his head and looked at me. I could not read his expression, but when I turned to leave, he said, "Whatever you want."

## II

The thought of Martin stayed with me after I'd left him at the food court, through the walk home, my encounter with Stone and hearing his recollections of the war, and then my capitulation about the party. And while I got ready to sleep, I felt Martin's presence still with me under the warm quilt as I read and turned out the light an hour later. I lay awake a long time as the night's wind howled along the yard outside my window and I wondered what our meeting meant for my future. For the first time in weeks it did not seem cloaked in inertia or uncertainty. I could see a time when we'd be a team, helping each other, making a life together. I decided I would go the next day to the university and try to see Martin, or if he wasn't there to set up a time to meet.

· · ·

In the morning, I avoided Celeste and Stone, whom I could hear in the kitchen, speaking to each other. I wore the blue sweater my mother had knitted for me during her chemo treatments, a sweater that brought out the blue of my eyes, and I put on makeup and pulled my hair into a high ponytail. When I retrieved my coat, scarf and boots from the closet by the front door and was putting them on, Celeste came up behind me. "Melanie. Where are you off to? Aren't you going to have any breakfast?"

"Thank you, Celeste. I'll grab something on campus."

"Not even a coffee?"

I put on a boot, stood, turned to her and saw she was looking at me with suspicion.

"You'll be home though, for supper. I mean no more staying out and upsetting him." She did not say this as if it were a question but rather an accusation.

"Really, Celeste. It's my choice to go out, but yes, I should be home by dinner."

"Good," she said before turning back to the hallway that led to the kitchen. "Besides there's talk of a terrible snowstorm starting tonight."

◆ ◆ ◆

There was a long, narrow room off the main office of the English Department, where a coffee urn had been set up, a small refrigerator, and water dispenser. On the opposite side of the counter which housed these items was a series of pigeonholes where messages and notices for staff and graduate students were placed. There was a note from Professor Edison in mine, saying she'd like to see me, and one from Joni. And while I was reading these notes, which were written by the department secretary on sheets from a telephone notepad, my eyes saw the cubbyhole for Martin's mail. It was hard to miss as a magazine and a series of those same yellow notes overflowed it. I stood for a moment and knew what I would decide to do in that instant—to look at his mail or not—would mark me as a certain type of woman. The abundance of his messages I reasoned, could easily have tumbled out of their resting place and then I would have been forced to pick them up and return them to where they should be. This was part of my thinking when I picked up the items and leafed through them. There was a magazine on Canadian literature, four messages from Professor Edison saying she wanted to see him, and at the bottom of this pile was a message from the secretary. It had been transcribed the day before, at the same time as Martin was in the library with me. It had a tick beside the square for "Please call", and the caller was listed in the hurried script of the secretary, a hand-writing I knew well. She had written, *your wife.*

I dropped the sheet as if it were hot. *Your wife.* I heard someone in the hallway and rushed to pick up the note and shove it back in the slot with the other sheets and magazine. *So he had a wife.*

Did I have a right to feel betrayed? I left the department and decided I did not want to see him, that I had no idea what I would say, and that instead I would return to Winter Willow. As I walked, quickly, head down, I thought how I could go back to my life with Stone until I had enough money to move out. I could handle that. These were the thoughts coursing through my mind as I passed students on the sidewalks without glancing up. That, and the thought I could forget Martin, that nothing had happened, a talk in the lounge, a meal in a crowded, decidedly unromantic hall, that there was merely a possibility of something happening, but that I could stop it now, before it mattered. The fervor of these thoughts should have warned me that it would not be so easy.

# 12

When I tried on the dress for the party a week later, I found I needed to shorten the straps. Throughout the house there was a sense of harried activity that I'd been avoiding all day, but in search of a needle and thread I went to the kitchen looking for Celeste. When I found her, she was helping to bring down a pile of dusty dishes from a high shelf, dishes which had most likely not been touched in over a decade. There were at least six people in the kitchen with her, cutting and placing flowers in vases, making hors d'oeuvres, slicing cake into bite-size pieces, arranging cheese and grapes on platters. "Oh Celeste, there you are, I was wondering…"

"What is it Melanie? What do you want?" she said. "You can see how busy I am." When I asked her for a needle and thread she muttered her annoyance as she searched through the drawers, returning with a spool of black thread, a needle wedged into it. "Here," she said and turned back to the activity of the room.

In my room, I shortened the straps, sewing quickly with tiny slip stitches, as my mother had taught me years before. *There*, I thought with satisfaction as I finished, shimmied into the dress and looked at myself in the mirror. And what did I see? It was a hurried glance, a quick reapplying of lipstick, combing my long hair down my back, and then turning away. But what I would give now to be able to see that young woman in the mirror from so many years ago.

There is a photo of me somewhere in this house, in a drawer or slipped into a book, lined up in a bookcase, a photo which was taken that night. My daughter found it and thought I looked comical, as if I were attending a Halloween event. "You look like a flapper," she said and because she was a young teenager at the time and I had no idea how she'd know about flappers, I laughed in response.

◆ ◆ ◆

The first people to arrive were Gavin and his wife, Edie, a woman likely younger than he was, a woman with an infectious laugh who always seemed primed and delighted to use it. She was an attractive brunette, thick coral-coloured lips with wide-spaced chocolate brown eyes and was what my mother would have called thick-boned. And yet there was something delicate about her deportment, about the way she sipped her wine and spoke with me. I liked her immediately. Shortly after she and Gavin arrived, there was a sudden influx, with at least twenty people in the foyer, shedding their coats and bending over to take off their boots. Plastic trays had been laid out for the overshoes and boots and Celeste and another woman hired for the occasion were taking the coats to the kitchen where a rack had been set up. The house was full of commotion, a gaiety that I saw reflected in Stone, who stood greeting friends, leaning toward the women in order to kiss their cheek, exhibiting a graciousness I'd never seen him display before.

Everyone in the room was older than me. They stood in groups, sometimes a laugh would break over the din from glasses, plates, the rustle of movement and conversations. A string quartet played on a riser at the far end of the room, its music melding into the background. I saw some of the older English professors who worked at the university or were professors emeriti, and when Stone went to introduce me to Professor Warren, the department head, he said, "Oh, I know Melanie already."

"Of course, that's right," Stone said. "It seems, Roger, that you were not very kind or fair to Miss Schofield recently."

Professor Warren avoided looking at me, "Couldn't be helped," he said.

"Oh, yes, I think it could have been helped." Stone then put his arm through my arm and said, "Well, all I can say is, your loss is my gain."

I loved Stone at that moment, when the department head looked away and said something about having to find his wife before stepping back from us. "Stone," I said when he was gone. "I don't know if that was a good thing to say."

"Oh, hell, Melanie, who do these men think they are? He could have been kinder. He could have been more helpful." So this is what Stone thought of the way I'd been dealt with by the English department, what he gleaned from the situation, that I'd been mistreated by them and that he disagreed.

"I should thank you."

"No, no need," he said. An older couple, carrying their wine glasses and smiling, approached us and he introduced me to them as his secretary. "Melanie, I have known Joe here since we were together at university and then later when we went to war together. A long time ago now, wasn't it, Joe?" he said, and the man turned to look at me. He put out his hand, but I noticed his smile slightly fade and he did not speak until I took his hand in mine, when he said, "Remarkable."

When I said, "Excuse me?" Stone interrupted by saying there were other people there from his university days, and how wonderful it was to see everyone.

. . .

When I left Stone to get another glass of wine, I saw Professor Edison standing with a man I assumed to be her husband. Within the larger group, they stood isolated in what appeared to be a conspiratorial union. She was dressed in the same type of dark suit she wore in the English department and was straining to see who was standing in the circle that surrounded Stone. As I watched her, Gavin's wife Edie came up beside me. "It's good that you're here," she said. "Stone needs you."

"Needs me?"

"You know what I mean," she said, but I didn't. Before I had a chance to question her, she saw someone in the crowd, waved to them, and excused herself.

By the wine table stood two women who were, I reasoned, two decades younger than Stone, the same age as Celeste and the wives of some of his old friends or colleagues, people he'd met when he was in his sixties and they were in their forties.

"It's barely changed," one of the women said. She was dressed in a grey gown, its fabric had silver thread woven throughout, a dress that matched her hair, twisted in a high bun at the back of her head. The subtle gown and hair were in marked contrast to her ruby red lips, a smudge of which was on her front tooth. The other woman had a wild mane of blonde-grey hair that circled her face and she wore a short black dress that revealed thick-kneed legs and large feet. These women were huddled so closely together, so intent on their conversation, that they did not notice me standing close by.

"Gregory thinks Stone has invited us here to say goodbye."

"Really, why would he think that?"

The woman with the red mouth said something I could not make out, something that made the other woman laugh and say, "Still those were the days, weren't they? I remember being so intimidated by him, I couldn't speak."

"Me too. But we were younger then—imagine—he seemed so old, though probably he was younger than we are now."

"Strange how that goes." They fell quiet. The woman with the red lips turned the stem of her wine glass in the palm of her hand, the concentration on her face telling me there was something more she wanted to say. "My God, he must be at least in his mid-eighties by now."

"He looks okay, well, maybe a bit frail. But when I was with him just now, he remembered the first time we met. He remembered that I spilt a glass of wine on that writer, what was her name?" the woman in the black dress said, then stopped, looked toward the ceiling, trying to recall the name. "Anyway, he talked about that and how mortified I'd been. So his memory is still intact."

"I know, but from what Edie said, he's rallied for tonight."

"The house has remained charming if a little dusty," the woman in black said, but her face had the look of studied attention as she tried to remember the writer's name, and so a few moments of silence fell when they both stood looking out to the room. "But I wonder what it's like with all this space and just two people living here."

"Oh, haven't you heard? There's an assistant now, a young thing. She's here somewhere, dressed in this strange get-up, a dress that looks like it's from another era."

*Really? This is what they thought?* These women who looked harmless, even kind. An itchiness spread up my spine and I longed to change from the dress, but instead I stayed, feeling indignant and wondering if I did in fact look as foolish as this woman thought. They both bent slightly to cover their laughing.

When she straightened, the woman with the red lips said, "Have you seen Celeste?" She turned to her friend, her eyes widening. "I saw her when I came in, looks like she's aged fifty years. I swear. And to think we were friends. I even introduced her to Stone. And now she won't even look at me."

"I haven't seen her, but by the sounds of it I might not have even recognized her. Whatever happened to her and Stone's wife, the second one? If memory serves, they were very close but then there was some kind of controversy, wasn't there?"

"No, that was the third wife, Ruth something-or-other. She was a strange duck, an artist I think."

"But I thought the one who left with the other writer—God, I'm having difficulty with names lately—I thought she was his first," the woman with the wild mane of hair said.

"He married young, when he was living in England."

"I didn't know that."

"Yeah, Edie said she was the love of his life. She thinks he never got over losing her," the woman with the red lips said, taking a sip of wine and looking out into the room.

• • •

As a result of my listening so intently to these women, I did not see or hear Professor Edison come up beside me. "Melanie. Here you are." I jumped slightly at the sound of her voice and the two women looked over and quickly left their place by the table. I reached around Professor Edison, poured a glass of white wine, and took a gulp.

"I was surprised to get an invitation," she said. "Was that you?"

"No. I had no say on who was invited."

"Well, that's strange. I don't know Stone Shackelford," she said. She was looking past me to see if she recognized any of the other guests. "I know his work of course." When her gaze rested back on me she said, "You look pale, Melanie. Is there something wrong?"

"No. I'm fine." Her puzzled look stayed, as she came closer to me. "I'm enjoying myself actually," I added quickly, my voice sounding defensive. I felt her sudden closeness as an invasion. With a final gulp, I finished the wine and was about to leave, when I remembered the plagiarism case against her about which Martin had told me. I was curious also to know if she'd seen Martin that week, if there was a reason he had not contacted me. But I knew if I mentioned him directly she would find it strange, so I decided to ask about her husband and see if she'd tell me anything about the case pending against her. "Was that your husband I saw you with earlier?"

"Yes," she said, her voice was harsh, as if I were interrogating her. She turned then to the table and poured herself a glass of wine. "We've been married a long time," she said, unrelated to anything I had said. "I really don't know what I'd do without his support. It's times like this you know who you can trust."

What did she think I knew? Certainly not enough to answer these statements with insight. So I merely nodded and said, "Well I guess that's good. I mean having a long marriage." But as the silence became oppressive, I put my wine glass on the table, looked at her directly, and decided it was not the time to ask about the case against her or about Martin. Being so close, I felt a sudden wave of sympathy for her. I noticed a redness around her eyes that made them look sore and told her that I'd see her next week. "At the university," I clarified and turned to leave.

"Yes, next week." She was confused perhaps even hurt, I could see that. I left before she could ask about the progress of my thesis, something I was sure she would mention if I stayed any longer, and climbed the stairway to the second floor. People were standing on the steps, in the foyer, and the hallway leading to the salon. I walked past them, recognizing no one.

. . .

In my room, the talk and music and laughter were muffled but hung in the air as if originating in a distant space, as if it were a private memory from a long time ago. Sitting on the side of the bed, I could see myself in the full-length mirror across the room. The image stopped me. There I was as the world saw me, a young woman, sitting in an ornate room, unsure of herself, unsure of the future, her blonde hair falling across her face, the gown shining blue and bright. I thought then of Martin, I thought how badly I wanted him there with me.

I undressed, hanging the gown in the cupboard with my other clothes—a corduroy jumper, a pale blue silk blouse that had belonged to my mother, skirts, a few sweaters folded on shelves or hung on hangers. I was never to wear the dress again, and when I'd see it— moving or sorting through my wardrobe, I'd remember the woman in the grey gown with the red lipstick and remember too what she had said in her conspiratorial tone to the other, forgotten woman.

I lay on the bed and listened, recalling the evening with Martin, until I heard the noise of people departing, the door opening, closing, again and again, until the sounds quieted, and I fell into a restless sleep.

# 13

The week following the party, Winter Willow fell into what was now a familiar pattern as Celeste, Stone and I lived together but saw little of each other. I still spent hours with his archives, placing them in chronological order, sorting them by topic, but any urgency was gone, and I no longer tried to see if there was anything in his records that pertained to his time in London. The routine gave me free time to read, which I did mainly in the downstairs library. Despite the fact that Professor Edison had said she'd see me during the week, I was unable to contact her, and while I waited for Professor Warren to assign a new supervisor, interest in my thesis slackened even more. Talk of bringing back the writing assistance program reached me when I went to the university in the middle of the week, but I told the assistant department head, a serious, nervous man visiting from a German university, who approached me about returning to my previous position, that I was not interested. "Ask one of the younger students. They're not disenchanted yet," I said to him when he stopped me in the hallway outside his office.

He frowned, and I could not tell if he was perturbed or confused. "I don't understand," he said. "They said you'd come back."

"Well, they, whoever they are, are wrong."

I was in the English department to check what was happening with regards to my supervisor and then return and pick up books from the library. While I did this, I kept thinking of Martin and even though I tried to appear as if I were not looking for him, after three hours, when I had not seen him, I felt disappointed. The inconsistency in my thinking was not lost on me, and to myself I admitted I needed to either plan to meet him, or actively forget him. The truth is from those first moments in the library lounge, I had begun a relationship with Martin and there was little that could stop that momentum. This is what fascinates me now, how love can grow in the most arid of environments, how it can survive for years and how life with its routine and plans and regrets cannot ultimately change the way a person feels.

. . .

Much as overcast weather moves in and stays for a protracted period of time, I felt a paralysis, making any endeavour seem overwhelming, when everything was touched by a lethargy and inexplicable dread. No longer did I think of Katherine Mansfield walking the heath, in her sensible woolen skirts and blunt haircut, her mind humming with images and words. Or Virginia Woolf writing on the board fashioned for her by her husband, Leonard, the room alive with her fevered imagination. I was reading current novels and short stories by Canadian writers, *Bear* by Marian Engel, Alice Munro's *Something I've Been Meaning to Tell You*, work I knew I did not have to approach with the same academic intensity as those books I read for my thesis. If I'd thought about it, I'd have known the way I was living, its aimlessness, was a way of hiding away, of letting the season's claustrophobia consume me, but I did not think about it.

. . .

At Winter Willow I usually worked in the library, either on the first or second floor, but one day, when I had spent most of the morning reading in my room, I became restless and went to the first floor, avoiding the library. I could not hear either Celeste or Stone and seeing it was the middle of the afternoon, reasoned they could be sleeping or occupied with some other quiet activity.

I went into the salon on the opposite side of the staircase from the first-floor library, the room where the party had taken place a week earlier. I had no reason to be there, a fact I knew both Celeste and Stone would remind me of, if they'd seen me, or rather, if they'd caught me. The chairs and two long sofas, facing each other before the large fireplace, were once again draped with cloths. In the middle of the ceiling a high chandelier hung, something I'd not noticed on the evening of the soiree when the room was crowded with people. I stood transfixed and wondered about all the things that had happened beneath that chandelier over the years. By the wall beside the door there was a large uncovered desk, a desk that had been removed before the party but was now back in its original spot. When I opened its drawer, it made a loud screech that shocked me with its discordant sound. I stopped to make sure neither Stone nor Celeste had heard the drawer open.

At the bottom were files, on top of which were two blackened candlestick holders and an assortment of threadbare doilies. I moved the objects off the papers and saw near the bottom of the pile one marked "London, 1922". I took the file, moved the fabric from a straight back chair by the door and sat down to sort through the documents.

Under a military release form and other official seeming papers was a photograph of Stone with his fellow servicemen, or so I assumed. It was difficult to know which of the young men in the photograph was Stone, as they were all dressed in the same type of uniform with their faces shadowed by the grey light of the day, further obscured by the fading black and white processing of the photo. There was a static quality to the faces, as if the photographer had caught them in an unguarded moment. On the back was the date October 1917 with their names and beside the name *Thomas* was the word 'dead' in brackets.

I was putting the photo back in the file to return it to the desk when I saw beneath, on heavy paper, the pinched handwriting of

Stone. Currently his writing was looser, wilder and shakier, but I could still recognize the handwriting on that paper—the large looped 'j' and 'g'—as coming from him. And so, I sat back in the chair to read.

> *My dear Catherine,*
> *We have been apart now more than a year, and I think of you still living in our apartment in Hampstead, still friends with people who had been our friends, still working for the university. Your sweetness, that aura that surrounded you, that attracted people to you, that would still be intact, I'm sure. Even though my memories now of our home, the overgrown pathway from our apartment that led to the heath, where we walked each evening, are coloured by what happened to me, by what I can only refer to as the illness of war.*

I stopped and listened to the sounds of the house surrounding me. Only silence. I knew that reading this letter was a trespass into the most private moments of Stone's past, and knew too if he discovered me he would be enraged. But more than anything, I wanted to continue so I put my head down, determined to read the remaining text quickly.

> *And the happiness we'd known becomes replaced by the image I have of your face when your blonde hair fell over it that horrible night when I grabbed and pushed you against the wall, how the beauty of your face was stricken with worry, pain and finally fear. These are the memories I wish I did not own, and even more, I wish you did not possess.*
> *And so I come here, to this room, in the house where I grew up, a place you've never seen. I can hear my mother in the garden, ordering the gardener, and there are people in this house, busy with useful tasks. But not me. My sister, someone I'm sure you would like, is in the hallway; I can hear her humming. Since the winter I have stayed mostly in my room, venturing out only to*

*see the doctor, or my few remaining friends from university. It has been a cold winter, but today is one of the first spring days, warm enough for me to open the windows in my room and smell the fresh earth, the honeysuckle bush, and an unnamed smell, something from childhood, that reminds me of the pale sunshine of early spring.*

His description of the house made me think how full of life it must have been that day, with his mother in her garden, his sister humming in the upstairs hall, and Stone himself, young and in love with the wife he left behind. In comparison the heavy quiet of the day I sat in seemed to lean against me, coaxing a near somnolence in the calm afternoon light of that winter afternoon.

*The winter, which had seemed to hold me, has loosened its grip and so I feel free to contact you, and hopefully explain, in the flawed way I have come to understand it, what happened. Why I changed, making it impossible for us to be together. It is not enough to say that I am sorry, although I am, I need to try—as I am trying in my novel, as I tried when I would discuss it with my friends and family—to explain what it was the war stole from me, what still sits heavy on my heart.*

*Imagine, Catherine, those men like me, just boys really, imagine them living with that constant, cold terror, the only reliable companion they could count on to still be there when they woke from their dark sleep. They'd sink into despair even more treacherous than the thick ooze that awaited them over the top of the trench in no man's land, the hundred yards of mud the colour of milk chocolate where they might sink to their hips into the quagmire and fall easy prey to German snipers. Each man feeling in his heart that he would never again experience the embrace, the comfort of being home, feeling with an unshakeable conviction he would draw his final breath in that hell.*

Oh, how awful, I thought, looking up from the letter. I was tempted to not continue but so curious was I about how Stone would bring this back to his time with Catherine in London that I anxiously looked back to the sheets in my hand.

> *Even the lucky solider—and I was one—was sure a German bullet would find him. I'd seen it, seen friends laughing one moment and gone the next, and they were the lucky ones, to be gone so quickly. The unlucky would have been riddled with shrapnel from one of the enemy artillery shells that could fall day or night. It would cut and burn into the poor boy's belly like the blue flame from a sadistic welder's torch.*
>
> *And those left, fearing the white, ghostly clouds of mustard or phosgene gas oozing and rolling silent across no man's land in the night, carried by wind and gravity toward their trench as they slept. Not even the most fearful soldier could sleep with a gas mask pressed for hours on his face. So uncomfortable and dangerous were they that the soldier would risk inhaling the burning, choking gas, knowing that one deep breath would fate him to a cruel death, when he'd wake with the sensation of boiling tea being poured into his throat. If he was lucky he'd be able to stagger up the trench ladder where finally the fire from a German machine gun would end it all. But usually he'd die writhing on the wet plank floor of his trench, gurgling and choking, while medics and other soldiers could do nothing to save him.*

I was nearing the end of the letter when I heard a thud in what sounded like the hall outside the salon. I raised my eyes, could hear my heart pounding. I stayed utterly still, staring at the door, willing it not to open. After a minute or so when everything remained the same, I thought the sound must have been the mail with something heavy perhaps, falling through the slot into the vestibule. Of course, I reasoned, it was that time of day, so I went back to finish the letter.

*And all of this, all I saw, does not compare with the role I
played in the death of young German men. Men I knew even
then who were more like me than our commanders, caring about
the same things I cared for, having, perhaps, someone at home
that they loved as much as I loved you.*

*It's impossible and these are mere words. My dear Catherine
I must stop, I must return to these rooms, to the sound of my
mother in the back garden, the activity of the house on this May
day. I must let it go. And with it you, my dear.*

I quickly turned the page around, no signature. And obviously
he had not sent it, at least not this version. I looked up to the room,
static before me, except for the calm flow of the curtain above the heat
register. How horrible, I thought, how horrible that this had been
Stone's experience, and how dreadful that he could not express fully
to the person he obviously loved the most how it had devastated him.

A second sound in the hall stopped me, made me scurry to
replace the photo and letter, return the file and stand by the closed
door until I was certain I could return to my room undetected.

# 14

After dinner one night shortly after I found Stone's letter, when
Celeste moved about the kitchen, washing and stacking dishes, placing cutlery in drawers, her movements brusque with purpose, she
began to speak about Stone as he had been in his younger years.
Those were the years when he'd lived at Winter Willow with his
mother before Celeste herself lived there, when a sister had died. I
could tell by the revered tone of Celeste's voice, that this death had
brought a permanent sorrow to the lives of Stone and his mother.

"What about Stone's father?" I asked. There was a yellowed
photograph of his mother and father in a heavy frame on the desk
of the library. Stone had told me it was his parents' engagement
photograph and I noticed in the inscription below the image, the
year had been 1888.

"He died young, that's all I know," Celeste said, wiping the metal
trimmed table and catching the crumbs in her cupped hand. "His
mother raised him, and she was absolutely crazy about him." That
rang true to me. Stone had the kind of confidence that spoke of early
and sustained validation. "She was also crazy about Sonia, his sister,
but a little over a year after Stone's return to Canada, she died."

"Of what?"

"I've heard different things. I even heard that she killed herself.
But I don't believe that. That was a rumour started by those people
who said they were his friends." Celeste stopped her scurrying from

counter to table and was standing in the middle of the kitchen, its solemn light falling over her, shadowing her face. She was holding a dishtowel, looking at me. "All I know for sure was it changed them, the death of that girl. And Stone's war experience, I'm sure that had a role to play as well."

"How old were you when you moved here?" I said, then quickly added, "Are you sure I can't help?"

I'd asked when I first began to have meals in the kitchen if I could help with the cleanup, but Celeste said it was more bother to have someone trying to help who did not know where things belonged. "That's the last thing I need, someone messing up the order of my kitchen," she'd said.

She came to the table and sat down. "Well, let's see, I was in my thirties, and it was shortly after the war, 1947, I think. His mother was still here when I came." Celeste put her elbow on the table, rested her head on her closed fist. "She was a harsh woman, disliked me, I think, or maybe just hated having to have me here."

"So why did you stay?"

"Mostly I loved the salons he hosted, all the artists who came." She stood and walked to the window, looking out to the garden. "I was young then, loved the commotion, loved to dance actually," she said, returning to the sink, her back now to me. Celeste dancing seemed inconceivable. "He wasn't always like this, you know, he was happy or content at least," she said, her head tilting up toward the ceiling. "His first wife stayed in Britain after the war, and I heard she died, not sure of what, but then he married a second time and that wasn't a very happy union."

"What happened?" I said.

"At first it was okay, of course. I don't suppose he would have married her if he'd known she'd leave with a man who'd been his friend."

It seemed it would be fitting to me that his wife had not left but instead gone mad, for this was the underlying sense of this house, a madness kept at bay by routine. When I said something to that effect, something about there being a mad ex-wife living on the third floor, a Bertha Mason who was being looked after by Grace Poole, Celeste turned and gave me an angry look, annoyed perhaps that I interrupted her recollections, or that I'd alluded to a novel and characters she did not recognize. So I quickly added, "Well, I've heard sounds coming from the third floor. At night, if I can't sleep."

She turned back to face the sink, "It's an old house, it creaks."

"These sounds aren't creaks," I said but knew her silence meant she did not want to speak of the third floor and what she considered my delusions. "So what happened, I mean to the second wife?"

"She must have fallen out of love, I suppose. His writing demanded a lot of attention and she didn't like that."

"I know his work was highly regarded," I said.

"Yes, and because of that there were parties with all sorts of people coming and going." I watched her back and could see her head tilt downward, her chapped hands resting on the counter and she remained so still that I knew she was recalling those days when she was younger. "She did not deserve him," she said simply after a few moments, going back to her washing.

"You didn't like her?"

"Not for him. His mother hated her, and they fought constantly. I think Stone believes his wife killed his mother, because shortly after one of their fights, his mother died. Died upstairs. In the room beside the library, your room, in fact."

"Is that when she left? His wife I mean."

"No, not right away. But he grieved, and they stopped speaking. He couldn't even write, and she couldn't stand the quiet, so she ended up leaving with that man." Celeste turned and looked at me as if at that moment she remembered to whom she was speaking and of what she was confiding. "This is a matter of public record, you could check it out at the library. I'm not saying anything not already documented." This sudden reluctance to speak had happened before, when Celeste would quickly move from recounting some past occurrence in a tone of glad reminiscence, camaraderie even, to a tone of recrimination, her voice sharp and accusatory, as if I had pried the information from her and she had succumbed unwillingly.

In the past she had told me about Stone's wives—Catherine, who had stayed in England and whom she had never met, the second wife—and that was the only way she ever referred to her, as 'the second wife'—who left with his friend, and a third who had contracted a virus and died in the winter of 1952. This third wife, Ruthy, was Celeste's favourite, and when she spoke of her it was always with a sense of wistfulness. "Life would have been so much better if she had lived," she said one day, looking out the back window, turned from me. And I knew she was probably thinking, *for one thing, you most likely would not be here.*

＋ ＋ ＋

It began one night when Stone tapped on the door to borrow a pen and then asked if I had a copy of *The Bostonians*, by Henry James. I was in bed reading and felt exposed and vulnerable in my nightgown, but I quickly gave him a pen from the side table and told him I did not own the book he wanted, even though there was a good chance it was in one of the boxes I had not yet unpacked. He thanked me and left.

The night before, I'd woken to sounds which seemed to be coming from the third floor, first a scraping sound as if someone was dragging furniture and then a thud. After Stone left my room, I remembered hearing these sounds, adding to my apprehension, and when I couldn't sleep, I lay there pondering how I could best protect myself from Stone's future visitations.

＋ ＋ ＋

In the next few weeks he visited six or seven times, always after I'd fallen asleep. I'd feel the bed shift as he sat on it. He'd put his hand to my face or run it along my hair. At first these visits had an unreal quality, as if part of a dream, as though his coming to my room was part of my sleep. If I'd been deeply asleep and his touch woke me with a start, he would rise from the bed quickly and leave, closing the door gently behind him so that I would be left to wonder if the visit had truly happened. Today I find it inconceivable that I let Stone come to my room, touch me so softly, but through a mixture of misplaced sympathy and obligation and an assumption that I could not stop him, it continued. Whatever it was—and looking back I still have difficulty saying with certainly why, but it is true—I let these nocturnal visits happen.

One morning after such a visit from Stone, I saw grey hair on the pillow beside mine and I wondered how long he had been there. It gave me a feeling of revulsion and then I became angry, mostly at myself for my complicity in allowing these visits to continue. Living with these two peculiar people, allowing Stone access to the most private moments of my day, would have been unimaginable just weeks before. And now approaching the end of winter, they hemmed in my life, as did Winter Willow with its dull light that stretched weakly into the rooms in waves of greyness.

In the kitchen I poured myself a bowl of cereal and was sitting alone looking out to the frozen garden when Stone arrived. "Melanie, my dear," he said, and I knew his voice well enough to hear in it a tone of excitement. "Just now I've received a letter from the university." His rushed voice continued. "They asked me to be part of some kind of conference on Canadian writing from the early twentieth century."

"Really," I said, putting milk on the cereal in my bowl, unimpressed and wondering if he really thought he was up to the rigour of presenting a paper and being part of a conference. These thoughts were cold and came to me from the distress I felt after finding his hair on my pillow.

"So I need you to go there, give them my acceptance." He was still dressed in his pajamas, covered by a robe, the belt dragging behind him. "This is how it was done in my time, and I think it shows a certain respect. I think they'd expect that from me, so please Melanie, you must go this morning." Did he really think, rather than a phone call to confirm, it made his position seem grander, or more formal, if his assistant accepted in person? *Next, he'll be wanting me to answer the door,* I thought bitterly.

"Here it is, my acceptance," he said and handed me an envelope. I looked at it, at his shaky handwriting. He had written the university address but no contact.

"Who's organizing it?" I said. "I may know them."

"Doesn't say. You need to go there." He left the room, his belt trailing.

What I needed, I thought, was to get away, to escape. I knew this since seeing his hair on the pillow that morning. Celeste came into the kitchen and seeing the milk container on the table, grabbed it and put it in the refrigerator without speaking. I finished my cereal and went back to my room, leaving the kitchen's oppressive silence.

There was so little of what was mine in that room, my books still in boxes packed when I moved from my rooming house, even my clothes filled only half the drawers and closet. Surveying, I thought how my things, which had been mine for years, no longer felt personal or worth owning. I went downstairs, put on my coat, stuffed my satchel with books and the note from Stone. When I left, I did not say goodbye to either him or Celeste.

The sky and my mood lightened as I neared the English department. What a bitter season this had been and continued to be, each day seeming colder than the previous. At the office of the English department, when I asked about the conference, I was told in a distracted way by one of the graduate students to go to a room on the floor below, which was where he believed the planning committee met. I was now hot. My hair and clothing made me warm so that when I got to the office where I was told to go and it was closed, I took my coat off and held it. I saw the agenda for the conference on the near-by bulletin board and as I was reading it, Martin came up behind me. "I did that."

"What?"

"I did that. Put Stone Shackelford on the agenda."

Unnerved at seeing him, and at the unexpected calmness of our exchange, I said, "Why would you do that?"

"If I'm being honest, mostly to see you." Our conversation stalled here with both of us looking at each other without speaking. He came closer, took my coat. "Come in. This is my office." The room was full of paper and books scattered on the floor and when I looked around for a place to sit, he said, "This mess is a sign I can tolerate ambiguity."

"What? What are you saying?"

"It's a sign I don't need order. That should make you glad." He placed my coat on the clothes hanger in the corner of the office.

"Why would that make me glad?"

"Because it means I don't expect everything to be neat, in its place, that I can tolerate messiness." When I gave him a look of barely concealed annoyance, he said, "For some reason, I have a feeling that would be important to you."

"I don't think you have any idea, Martin, what is important to me." He moved behind his desk, sat watching me, quiet until I said, digging through my backpack to find the acceptance, "Here's Stone's, I mean Mr. Shackelford's, acceptance." I was standing and when he did not accept the envelope, but instead stared at me in a thoughtful way, I placed it on his desk.

He took it from where I'd put it, motioned for me to sit and ripped it open. He read the note and then looked up at me, saying in a slow voice, "Stay, Melanie. I really want to speak with you. I know you don't have any obligation, that you don't even know me, but I am asking for you to stay and listen."

I was alert and watchful, seeing for the first time the earnestness that would in the years to come always convince me to do what he asked.

I sat down and said, "You're married."

"How did you know that? Because that's what I want to tell you. It's what I wanted to tell you at the food court that night."

"And why didn't you?"

"It seemed, I don't know, presumptuous."

"Why, because you were engaging me in a way that can only be described as flirtatious?"

"No. Because it was as if I was inferring you were interested in me that way. And that just seemed too fast, or something."

I was seated before him and saw his concern, how it had erased his smile, saw how it darkened his features. "I tried to call you, but whoever answered the phone said you did not live there."

"Really? Was it a man or woman?"

"Woman, became quite angry at me at one point. So then when I was working on this conference, I thought Shackelford could fit the agenda."

"Why were you trying to contact me?"

"Why do you think, Melanie? I wanted to explain to you that my wife and I do not live together. We're not even in the same city." I wondered then—watching him lean on the desk toward me, so that his blue eyes, their intensity and concern, seemed to fill the space between us—if I could believe him.

◆ ◆ ◆

When I returned to Winter Willow it was with the taste of Martin in my mouth. I thought to push him away when he bent to kiss me, but did not, so curious was I about how that kiss would feel. And I knew if I'd pushed him away, I would regret it. When I entered the back porch of Winter Willow, I was thinking this, how risky it had been, and yet how insensibly happy I felt.

Stone was waiting for me in the hallway off the kitchen. "So?" he said. "What's the conference about? Did you get a synopsis?"

I had forgotten to enquire about Stone's role in the conference, so I said, "The agenda is not formalized yet". Stone pursed his lips and looked at me critically.

He put his hand to my hair, smoothing it. Stepping closer, his face before me in close orbit so that I could not look around it. I jerked back. "What is it? Why do you always move away from me?" he said.

At that moment Celeste came from the kitchen, drying her hands on her apron. "You missed lunch," she said.

I looked at Stone, then Celeste, who were both irritated, and it occurred to me that my presence in this house had changed everything for them. I'd been thinking only of my situation when I decided to live at Winter Willow, but the experience of living there, while changing so many of my assumptions about Stone, must have also destroyed the balance between him and Celeste. In the past something likely took place to strand them both there, where they intersected only briefly each day and spent the rest of their hours in their quiet rooms occupied with their private pursuits.

"I need to rest," I said to Stone, who moved aside, allowing me to pass him and reach the stairs.

As I neared the landing for the second floor, he called to me, "I've left a copy of *The Uninvited* on your bedside table so that you could reread it." *Why now*, I wondered? Had he merely forgotten to give it to me as he'd promised, or did the invitation to present at the conference awaken his memory of the writer he'd been?

"Yes. Thank you. I will." And yet I did not reread his novel, not for many years anyway. I wonder if this reluctance was an attempt to not be swayed in my knowledge of Stone, not influenced by the words which had led to his privilege and relevance. Or was my lack of curiosity just another example of the inertia that had befallen me since moving to Winter Willow?

In my room, I noticed how the day had finished its final descent into night and even though it was not yet six p.m., I could see a flat, dimensionless dark pressed against the window between the curtains. My thoughts were occupied by Martin and how in his office he'd told me he and his wife had decided to separate. She not only agreed, he said, but was, in fact, happy they would be starting new lives.

He told me they'd discussed it over the phone because she was still living in Philadelphia where they had lived and attended university together. He had transferred to my university because they'd decided to take a break from their marriage. And meeting me, he said, feeling what he did, helped to clarify that it was the right thing to do. She would stay there, and he would stay living with the group of graduate students with whom he'd been staying. He told me all this happily as if it resolved all complications, but I did not believe it would be this easy.

The wonder—and it was nothing less—that I felt when he leaned over me, his mouth finding mine, was stifled when I arrived home, saw Stone, and felt his eagerness to learn what I'd been told. In my room, I thought how it was possible that what Martin had said about his wife's willingness to end their marriage, his caring for me, might not be true—not a lie, exactly, or at least not a deliberate one, but something that would not withstand the scrutiny of time. I thought how it was possible that my desire to meet Martin again, to have him explain his relationship with his wife had made me complicit in the story, eager to accept it as truth. I realized that's how delusions often start, as a want or a need. I crawled into bed hugging a pillow and rocked in time to my thoughts.

"Melanie," I heard Stone in the hall. "Are you all right?"

"Yes, just tired."

"Well, dinner's in half an hour." I heard him leave my door and shuffle down the hall to his room.

When I closed my eyes an image of my mother on the morning bus rose before me. Often I was with her then, when I'd see her place her purse on her lap, her hands, in white gloves, over its clasp, her attention locked outside the window, as streets and sidewalks and the assortment of commuters slid by. What I would give now to be able to sit beside her, say something to make her turn her head and look at me.

What would she think of these people that hemmed in my life

now, people she'd never met. Together we'd lived a closed life, with only the two of us in our small apartment. She had a brother, my uncle, but they'd lost touch and she seldom mentioned him. I thought how for her the void of his absence would have had a shape, a negation. "You and me, kiddo," she'd say at night when I was young, putting me to bed, and I'd feel as if this was the way it should be. Just her and me. But at that moment in Stone's house, I wondered what it meant for her to have family she no longer knew, to have memories in the shape of rooms she no longer entered. And I wondered if her concern for me, the way she questioned my decisions, asked about friends, school projects, teachers, the way all this could be viewed as a desire for control, but was really somehow an attempt to counter her loss of family.

Drawing closer to sleep, I thought with a sudden urgency what Martin had told me about his phone calls being kept from me, and I jumped up to a seated position. I left my room, walking determinedly down the front stairs to the kitchen. There I found Celeste bent over, removing buns from the oven. "Celeste, a friend said he'd been trying to contact me." She looked at me with annoyance. "And he said someone, a woman, told him I did not live here."

"Impossible," she said, resting the hot tray on the counter.

"Well, that's what he said, and regardless, I am requesting if I do get a call, to please let me know."

"Melanie," she turned to me, her oven-mitted hand on her hip. "There has never been a call for you here, and besides, when has my job come to mean being your personal secretary." She gingerly picked up the buns and placed them in a basket, then turned her back to me as I left her and went back to my room.

•  •  •

When I went downstairs for dinner and entered the kitchen again, Stone was seated, wearing his suit and tie, the formal clothes he always wore. *You are an ornate bird*, I thought, *and just as foolish*. He stood when I entered and when I sat he bent and kissed my fore-head, as a father might an obedient child. Celeste turned from the stove to witness this new and, to my mind, bizarre move, and I saw her expression freeze. She was carrying a casserole dish and had to steady herself so as not to drop it. But her look before she placed the hot dish on the counter, the look she aimed at me was one of cold hatred, pure and revealing. And yet had she not always encouraged me to be compliant to Stone? to see to him when he was upset? to cater to his whims?

I had come to consider Celeste, like myself, a satellite in Stone's orbit, each of us occupying separate spheres of influence and ser-vice, but her look told me she considered my position now elevated to hers, that she had been somehow usurped by me. Her attitude confirmed, once again, that I should leave Winter Willow, leave the union of Celeste and Stone to play out its final scenes without me.

# 15

The conference agenda gave Stone twenty minutes to give a reading and answer questions. "I'd break it into ten minutes and ten minutes, and make sure someone is there to ask the first question," I told him. "I'd do it, but many people know I work for you."

"Do you honestly think there'd be no one there wanting to ask a question?"

I had said the wrong thing, so added quickly, "Of course not, but often people are intimidated or shy to speak, especially to a writer they admire. You must allow for that, Stone."

He softened, "Hum. Maybe."

We were proceeding as if Stone was well enough, focused enough, to give a lecture, but there were times when I wondered if it would happen, despite how being invited to present had given him a renewed vitality.

About the house, on bookcases, desks, anywhere that could accommodate them, were framed photographs from Stone's life or framed magazine and newspaper reviews. The photos showed a man accepting awards or giving lectures, but this was not the man I saw every day. He stumbled often, and at times his thoughtful expression would soften to an unfocused stare. He was failing, in health and thought. Had the dismal scenes of Stone having diffi-culty mounting the steps, leaning heavily on the railing, or slowly walking the hallway, feeling his way along the wall, become more common or had his frailty always been the case and I had never truly noticed before?

That Friday afternoon, there was to be a meeting for the organizers and other participants of the conference. Martin had called me to speak about it, a meeting Stone would have to attend, but before closing off he said, "You'll be here? We'll be able to talk I hope." I had not been to the university in a week, since the day I discovered he was the conference organizer, the day he told me he was leaving his wife.

"I'll be with Stone, but we won't be able to talk."

"Come on Melanie, we can't leave it this way."

"Martin, this is your decision. I can have nothing to do with it."

"Of course, but we have to speak. And besides, it's been decided. I told you."

Celeste came in the kitchen, looked at me crossly. I knew she considered this room part of her space and did not like me using the phone here or for that matter, being in the room at all except for mealtimes or entering the house. I turned from her and lowered my voice. "Listen. This is the problem. I'm not sure I'm up for this right now. I mean there's other things to consider, things I want to do, and I feel if we are together I would be replacing one problem for another and..."

He interrupted, "I'm a problem?"

"Of course you are, you're a huge problem, you must see that."

Despite what I said, when I worked in the library, or read in my room, it was always with the thought of Martin close by. I pictured the way he looked, remembered the things he said. Even after I'd stop myself, aim my thoughts at more immediate concerns, he was always there, his energy, his promise, a contrast to the sleepy paralysis of Winter Willow. "Oh, Martin, I don't know what more I can say." I looked down to the kitchen floor, to the white and yellow tiles, and heard Celeste open the refrigerator door. "Yes, I will see you, but we won't have much time."

We hung up. I realized as Celeste was busying herself at the counter, taking out a cutting board, knives, vegetables from the fridge, as the silence bloomed between us, that I was frightened to start a relationship with Martin, and I worried too about not having a relationship with him. I stood holding the phone, which now hummed with his absence, and thought how I could already sense the pain of losing him, as if it were a distant sound. It seemed inevitable, something growing there beside me. I was thinking this when I heard Stone on the stairs, "Who was that?" he said when he entered the kitchen.

"The university. There's a meeting tomorrow you have to attend for the conference."

"Good. Good. Where?"

I told him and then added, "But I don't have to be there."

"Oh yes, you do, for one thing you have to show me where to go."

I knew he'd say this and conceded without an argument. "All right, if you want. But I won't sit in."

. . .

The next day, Stone and I walked the familiar route to the university, and I thought as I noticed the sallowness of his skin, the way the colour of his hair and face had the same grey hue, that I had only seen him outside once, on the day we met. On the sidewalk he seemed even more frail, so as we walked, I put my arm through his.

At the office of the English department he handed his coat to the secretary, who stood when we entered. She looked at it and then me. I took his coat from her to hang it in the staff vestibule beside the door, in the hallway that led to the graduate students' offices. While I did this, I heard him say, "I'm Stone Shackelford, here for a meeting." I quickly put the coat on a hanger, dropped his overshoes, and hastened my return to the office, where I saw him standing in a regal pose, looking pointedly down at the secretary.

"Can you tell me where they're meeting?" I asked her.

She finished what she was typing and without looking up said, "The meeting is downstairs in the conference room. You know, Melanie. Beside Martin's office."

"Who is Martin?" Stone asked in the elevator. When its doors opened we could hear voices coming from the conference room at the end of the corridor.

"Another grad student," I said.

When we reached the conference room and Stone entered, everyone grew quiet. One of the older professors started to clap. The sound against the previous silence seemed stark, but then other people stood and joined in the clapping. Martin, seated near the back of the room, looked around when the sound began and then stood to clap as well. "Well, Mr. Shackelford, I think you know how we feel to have you here," he said, walking toward us. He shook Stone's hand but did not look at me.

I left the room, sure no one other than Martin noticed, and returned upstairs to check the mail in my pigeonhole. There I found notices of readings and book signings and a note from Professor Edison to all her students. She wrote that while the investigation into the 'hurtful' allegations issued against her continued, she would be on leave.

After reading the note I went back to the main office and asked the secretary, who was turned from me at her desk, "Do you have any idea how long the meeting will go on?"

She turned, looked over her glasses and said, "He has the room for two hours."

"If they break early, would you please tell Stone—Mr. Shackelford—I will return in an hour and a half from now, that'll be 11 o'clock."

She did not respond, kept typing and in a distracted way said, "Quite the loony, that one".

"What? Who?"

"Shackelford. He's seems not quite all there." She stopped typing, looked at me and smiled. "I mean, you must have noticed."

"Oh yes, I guess." I was anxious to leave. I'd missed the hours of quiet I'd spent in the library, the things that had made it a refuge and

as familiar as the space had been at the rooming house. But on my
way there, passing groups of students in the interconnecting tunnels,
hearing their rambunctious conversations, or watching the somber
progress between buildings of other, solitary students, I found her
words repeating. They made me feel angry, first toward her and then
at myself for not defending Stone.

I found an isolated seat, took my book, Virginia Woolf's diary,
from my satchel and began to read, folding my legs under me. It was
a cold day and I could hear the wind hitting the window. And yet as
I read, London in the early 1920s came into view, a meeting between
Virginia Woolf and Katherine Mansfield in Katherine's house in
Hampstead. The day was sunny and after a stilted start, the women
began to discuss their need for solitude, its role in their writing. Sun
on the window ledge, on the linen table cloth, the lemon-coloured
walls, provided the perfect backdrop for their interaction. In the
midst of their conversation, Katherine's husband entered the room,
interrupting them. Reading Woolf's entry, I was in that room, could
feel the sun's warmth on my arms, the lightness of a felt hat on my
head, wool stockings on my legs. This was where I was when Martin
interrupted me, much as John Middleton Murray had interrupted
the two writers so many years before.

"I knew I'd find you here," he said, as my view flattened to him
in front of me. Beyond him the blinding square of a window newly
whitened by falling snow came into view, erasing that sunny day
in London.

"Are you finished? Is Stone ready to leave?"

"No, we took a break and I said they could continue without me."

"But shouldn't you be there?"

"Yes, of course, but I need to speak with you."

I did not want to speak with him. I wanted to go back to that
room with the two women. And yet part of me wanted nothing more
than to speak to him. "Leave me be, Martin," I said and let my gaze
drift back to the book.

"I'm not leaving."

A student at a nearby desk said forcefully, "Please".

I closed my book and placed it in my satchel, grabbed my coat from the back of the chair and walked indignantly to the stairwell. There, in a voice that was not only loud but echoed, Martin said, "We can talk downstairs." The lounge where he'd told me about Professor Edison was crowded, but as we entered a couple vacated the same chairs where we had sat that night.

"I'll stop if you really want me to," he said when we settled.

"Can't you see this will lead nowhere."

"First," he said. "That's not true. But it can only lead somewhere if you want it to. You're the only true obstacle." What a handsome man he was, this thought struck me unbidden and annoyed me. "I must ask," he said. "Does it have anything to do with Stone?"

"Stone?" my voice tinged with indignation.

"Yes. He said something about you being his girl Friday. I think that's how he worded it, but it seemed like he meant to imply more."

"He means I'm his assistant, that's all." But I could feel an old antagonism toward Stone swell inside me. And then I remembered the grey hair on the pillow and how a week before I'd woken to Stone touching my head. When I jerked awake, he stood so I could see his confusion, the tufted hair, his long, slender feet, covered in slippers.

"There's something," Martin said, sitting back in his chair. "And I need to know."

"You don't need to know anything." My annoyance bubbled up inside me with a sudden icy certainty, when I said, "You have a wife, remember?"

He leaned back, and I thought how our conversations now tended to dissolve into these loops of recrimination and argument, after which the same facts remained. He was married—every time we'd met, even after our meeting that day, he would return to his routine where another woman was his wife, even if she was not living with him, a woman who knew him far better than I did, and whom he knew far better than he did me. And part of my life, the part he'd never know, existed in that house with Celeste and Stone. "Oh, Martin," I said, feeling defeated. "This is such a bad time for us to have met."

He sat back, looked around the room, out the window, where snow continued to fall. "I must get back," he said finally. "You too. It'll soon be over."

In the English department, the meeting had just broken up. I heard one of the younger professors say to Stone, "I read your book as a teenager. Nothing since then touched me as deeply." When I sidled up beside them and Stone took my arm, I could feel a tremble.

"Come on, my dear. This is quite enough excitement for the day. Time to go home." I retrieved Stone's coat, overshoes and hat as the professor followed us, continuing his story of how Stone's book impacted his life.

◆ ◆ ◆

When we were alone out on the street, walking back to Winter Willow, Stone said, "I told you. There was a time, there really was a time," his voice trailed away into a wistful tone. I could tell the session at the university had made him feel expansive; it had buoyed him in some fundamental way, even if the darkened skin under his eyes told me it had also taken a toll. I knew he was glad for the conference and for his role in it. But I felt a contrast between that lightness of mood and his stiff clutch of my arm, the shake in his grasp, and after these statements he remained quiet the rest of the way back to Winter Willow.

# 16

The night after our meeting at the university, Stone once again visited me in my bedroom. I heard the door open and felt his weight on the bed. I woke slightly to feel the essence of his being with me, but was too tired to fully wake. Until he leaned over me. "My dear?" he said. And I smelt something sour emanate from him so that I woke fully, in anger.

"Stone! You need to stop this." I sat up in bed.

"But look at how they loved me today. You must agree, Catherine, it was pretty wonderful."

"Catherine? Stone, do you even know who I am?" I pulled the quilt up closer to my face, forcing him to stand.

"Yes, of course," he said and turned. At the back of his head his hair was sticking out in a comical tuft, something I peevishly watched as he slowly moved to the door.

When he left, and the room settled again, and I drew the cover higher over me, unable to sleep, I thought of Martin, how I wished he were there. I wanted to feel his warmth, to feel his body, and as I rocked, I imagined the relief of making love to him. I needed to see him, to finish our conversation, and so I fell asleep hoping he would call on the weekend and resolved to see him the following Monday if he did not.

. . .

The next morning I told Celeste as she was sweeping the kitchen floor that I was expecting a call. "And if you hear it please let me know."

"How nice for you Melanie," she said as she bent to use the dustbin.

•  •  •

That weekend in late February, at the end of the month I always considered the worst of winter months, felt like an island of winter where time had stalled. On Saturday the weather fluctuated from a heavy snowfall to hours when only a series of stray flakes flickered before the window, between me and the trees, the distant houses, the consistently white-grey canvas of sky. Snow gathered like the inverse of shadows in the crook of branches, along the unplowed pathways, smoothed by yet another layer of the white meringue of snow.

I waited for the phone to ring but it remained as still as the garden sleeping under the weight of the storm. That night I had dinner with Celeste and Stone, a dinner where we barely spoke, after which Stone left abruptly, saying he needed to work on his talk. After the meal, I lay on my bed unable to concentrate on the book I was reading, instead I looked out at the trees, which stood ghostly, illuminated by the ambient light from the house, silently gathering snow. I wondered what Martin was doing and these thoughts, along with the storm's heavy silence, served to further slow time.

•  •  •

After the weekend, in which I only saw Stone and Celeste at meal-times and was otherwise alone, staying mostly in my room, listening for the ring of the telephone, I was anxious for Monday, determined to confront Martin. Another cold winter day greeted me the next morning when I opened the front door and quickened my walk to do just that.

. . .

He was not in his office when I arrived and the department secretary, who saw me walk by, called me back to say Professor Warren wanted to see me. She added, "Everyone is talking about how frail that crackpot you work for looked last week," before going back to her desk. "They don't think there's any way he's going to able to give a paper at the conference."

I ignored her and asked why Professor Warren wanted to speak with me. "He's worried about you losing the term."

"I was waiting for an advisor to be assigned," I said, but in truth I had barely worked on or thought of my thesis since hearing of the case against Professor Edison. I knew that at any other time I would have been anxious to have the issue resolved and would have pushed to have an advisor assigned.

"You should talk to him. I'll make an appointment for this afternoon," she said, looking at his agenda in a large leather-bound book on her desk. "Come back at two."

On the way to the library, I contemplated my thesis, and how important it had once been and how the thought of it had seldom been far from my mind. Now it seemed a distant concern, one about which I had to force myself to worry.

. . .

Early afternoon, I stood before Professor Warren's desk. "Interesting party at Shackelford's," he said. "So, how long have you been living there?"

"About two months, not long."

"You know, Melanie. We want you to succeed. It wasn't our aim to derail your studies. You need to know that."

"I know," I said. "It only feels that way."

He straightened, my comment creating an alertness in him, and to shift the conversation he said, "Please sit. So what have you been concentrating on lately?" His casual attire and ponytail contrasted with his deadpan tone, its inflection of efficiency and rigid judgment.

I ignored his question and said, "I'm feeling a loss of momentum in my thesis. Perhaps because I've lost two advisors as well as losing my funding."

"Well, you'll lose more than that; you'll lose your place at the university if you don't produce something soon. You know that, don't you?" He was annoyed, leaning sideways on the arm of his chair. "For God's sake, Melanie, this is your career we are trying to salvage here," he said.

I told him I would revive my research and start writing an outline for the thesis; I told him the winter had been fatiguing but that now at the end of February, I was sure my resolve and energy would return. When I said this, I was not sure I believed it. "I hope so, Melanie. For your sake." His glance drifted to the window, to a sky streaked with thin clouds like pulled angel hair.

"A PhD dissertation is not something you can do on the weekend," he said as summation. I was about to say that I agreed, that that had been my argument when he advised me to work and finish my thesis part time, but I felt chastised and weary and so said nothing.

◆ ◆ ◆

When I left his office, Martin was in the hall, leaning against the wall, reading. "Good. I've been waiting for you," he said when I appeared.

I felt dejected from my meeting but followed Martin to his office, where he turned and faced me. "My wife came here this weekend and we were able to speak." So this had been what he was doing, I thought, he'd spent the weekend with his wife.

"Did you know she was coming here?"

"Yes. No, not really," he said. "But what you need to know is we've come to an agreement we both can live with." He sat in the straight back chair close to the door, looking up at me, and I thought how young he looked and almost giddy with what he was telling me. "Really, she said she would have left if I hadn't."

I was not feeling the same lightheartedness that this news created in him and was only aware that while I was waiting for a call during that isolating weekend with its cold wind and snow, he'd been sharing the time with his wife.

We both grew silent, he because he could not understand my reluctance and I, because I was perturbed. After a few moments locked in this stalemate, I said, "How am I supposed to take the fact that you and she were together all weekend?" This was not what I wanted to say. I knew it made me sound needy and judging and yet it was said before I could contemplate its effect. When I saw his face slump with disappointment, I felt contrite. "I'm sorry, Martin," I said simply.

"You can't believe, can you? That something this good can happen." He tented his hands between his knees, his index finger pointed to the floor. "Look, all I'm going to say is regardless to what happens to us, my wife and I are separating. It's that simple—and has nothing to do with you." He stood, approached me, put his finger under my chin, drawing my face toward him, we kissed and then again, and again. Our lips plush against each other, the warmth between us, the initial tentativeness, the softness of his tongue on my lips, my tongue. I see now that this warmth was the cause of so much that was to come and was, I came to realize, more telling and more intimate than anything else that followed.

"I've left the apartment I shared, and yesterday I was able to move to a room in the student dorm," he said. I saw this for what it was, a cue to tell me we now had a place where we could be alone, and so without discussing it further, we buttoned our coats, wound our scarves around our necks, and left his office, crossing the barren central pathway, which in the coming months would be vibrant with summer colour, crossing to the squat buildings that overlooked the central quad, the buildings that housed the students' residence. Martin said, "Damn cold," as we drew close to the dorm, and I agreed, but other than that we did not speak.

In the bare room with its single bed, a utilitarian desk, a window with short curtains, a tall wardrobe with a long mirror, we threw our coats and scarves onto the floor and began again to clutch at each other, tentatively at first and then with intensity.

I was wearing a loose-knit sweater over a white T-shirt and once I had discarded my coat and we began to kiss, I raised my arms so that he could lift the sweater over my head—my hair dancing with static electricity. He removed his shirt and I could feel the skin of his shoulders, his chest, under my hands and wanted to feel it against the skin of my body. It was a deep urge, an opening inside me, of my being; it compelled me with its promise of pleasure, and I could do nothing except respond to it. Untethered to time, this need was an abandonment that contained its own logic, its own reward. I unzipped my skirt, removed it and my leotards, and stood then before him. He still had his jeans on but was bare-footed. It was cold. I hugged myself, and he stopped undressing to look at me. "Well, now. What luck is this?" he said and came forward, holding me as we moved toward the bed. There he put a sheet and blanket around me and rubbed my arms warm. Through a contorted effort he was able to remove his jeans, while I removed my underwear, undoing my bra so that I was now fully naked. We were both laughing and as there was not much space on the mattress, I moved on top, straddling him. The sheet fell, revealing me.

What was it that involved my heart that day, the overriding canopy of the mind and body? A want so fierce that I let it overtake me. When he touched me, layer upon layer of my skin was silenced with a soothing warmth. His body against mine—millions of spikes, like stars, alive and glittering, feeling like hundreds of hooks in my skin, holding me there. Moving into each other, there was a lightness, a discarding of the dense winter feel of my life from that time, from those quiet rooms of Winter Willow.

There is a hallucinatory feel to the memory of our first lovemaking—its rush and novelty overtaking us, but I do remember when the sounds and emotion quieted, we lay in each other's arms and laughed about the professors in the department, especially Helen,

whom Martin had labelled 'Nazi-head'. He told me about his childhood in Baltimore, in a working class neighbourhood, the red brick
buildings he lived in with his single mother. But unlike my mother,
she was usually depressed and spent whole days on the couch, asking
Martin to change the channel on the TV, and lamenting what a bad
mother she had been. "But really, she was the best she could be, and
besides it gave me such freedom."

He was playing with my hair, staring at the ceiling and I was
resting on his chest.

"I was always outside because it was just too dark in our
apartment."

"So how did you end up here? In this city? In Canada?"

"I always loved Canada. My grandmother lived in Montreal, and
I came often in the summer as a boy. But I liked the winter best. So
when I had the chance to come here, when my wife and I decided
to take that break, and there was a professor I could work with here,
well, I just jumped."

"And when did you get married?"

"She was a neighbour." His voice now terse. "We were so young."
I knew he didn't want to speak of his marriage. He stretched his arm
toward the side table, to turn the light on. "Let's go for Mexican," he
said. "I'm in the mood."

· · ·

Looking back on this day, I see it as a simple, common happiness.
Together, two young students, holding hands, in a crowd of other
students, loud music playing, everyone speaking, the sudden biting
sound of laugher and conversations. Over the noise, I could hear
Martin as he spoke of his mother who still lived in Baltimore, and
who called him every Sunday. "I told her about you".

"And what did you say?" The sun was lowering and there was a
golden light that stayed for a moment lighting the street, the cars,
passers-by on the sidewalk, the scene we could see out the restaurant

window. Soon it was replaced by the dark that stood as backdrop above the stores and restaurants, high streetlamps illuminated the walkways in a coned brightness, a light that fell quietly with the same density as the snow.

"I told her you were wonderful."

· · ·

When you love someone, you can always make them out in a crowd, the way they walk, turn their head. You can follow their eyes to whatever it is that has caught their attention: a store window display, the dancing homeless man, thick threatening clouds. For you the loved one will always be silhouetted against the monotony of any crowd— an aura about them, an isolating singularity. I thought about this when Martin left to go to the washroom and later headed back to our table through the busy restaurant. How full of amazement I was at the sight of him and wondered why there were so many people in the room who did not even turn to watch him pass.

· · ·

We ate fajitas as we continued the stories of our childhoods, how close my mother and I had been, how devastated I was by her loss. "When was that?" he said.

"Almost a year now."

"Poor Melanie," he said, and I looked down, so he could not see how his sympathy touched me, how it made me aware that I was a person in need of sympathy.

"Well, that's life, eh?" I said, and he put his hand over mine.

"I can imagine you as that little girl. I really can. And I love that child, just as I love you now." When I stopped and looked at him, I realized that I too could imagine him as the boy playing with friends in the alleyways and playgrounds of Baltimore, sitting on buses, the red-brick houses stacked in long streets gliding by its windows. And the image somehow quieted me, so that I could sense another life for myself, that other possibilities were opening up. I belonged in this restaurant, with these people, in the mood of jovial commotion. I belonged there, and the thought, along with the memory of our lovemaking, made me content in a way I had not been since moving to Winter Willow.

# 17

When I arrived back at Winter Willow, Celeste was at the front door waiting for me. She told me Stone had taken to his bed earlier in the day. "What happened to you?" she said. Her anger brought me up short and I stopped and really looked at her, at the drawstring pucker of skin around her pursed lips, the deep wrinkles about her eyes that were sparked with accusation. She saw my inquisitive gaze and said, "What? Why are you looking at me like that?"

As I took off my coat, removed my boots and placed them in the front closet, I said. "Just… why are you here anyway? What can it give you?" I turned, mounted the stairs but she followed, tugging at my sweater.

"Wait a minute. I want to know what happened."

"Do you really?" I said, turning to her, close now, so that I was able to see the colour of her light brown eyes. "Do you want to know how he comes to my bed some nights?" She pulled back, held her sweater tight to her throat. "Do you want to know how I sent him away this morning?"

She straightened, mustered a forced dignity and said in a whisper, "You know nothing." She spat the words and her eyes darkened with irritation. "When he was younger, when all the accolades were showered on him. You don't know how wonderful he could be, and how wonderful it could be living here." Through this encounter it became clear to me, witnessing her biting fury, how much she loved him and ultimately how inconsequential that love had become.

"You should leave here, Celeste. There's more to life." She turned without answering and descended the stairs, leaving me alone there. Again it struck me how I had upset the balance that saw Celeste and Stone living in this old rambling house in some strange equilibrium of need. She cared for him and Stone, distracted, never appreciating what she did for him, hungry for something from the outside world, an acknowledgment of his talent, his relevance, always overlooked her. I imagined the years full of days like the one I stood in at that moment, with its white winter light, making everything still, settling into each room evenly. Or the summers when the garden would be in bloom, that garden I had seen only grey and brittle. The thought of how all that time had played out, lay in silent layers on the rooms of that big sad house and how that silence had stopped me over the weeks I'd been there. And could it have been only weeks, when it seemed to me that I had lived a whole lifetime during that cold, cold season. What I'd encountered had shown me the way life can sink into disappointment so profound as to thwart a person's character. I was infused with the sense of failure that seemed to emanate from Winter Willow, and this sense, it struck me then, could only be closely aligned to the process and the sadness of growing old.

In my room, I paced. I felt as if a truth had been revealed that was the key to why I had ended up there and that made me strangely unresponsive. It was true I was too young to know what kept Celeste and Stone together. I had not come to that moment when the past becomes as real as the present. I had not yet known the sort of regret that Stone and Celeste must have lived with. I only saw his timidity, the way he kept away from the world, his sleepy head bent over notebooks in the library, dozing by the fire in the downstairs den during the afternoon hours, being woken by Celeste for dinner. I felt a strange mix of emotions—on one hand, pity for the waste and the sense of regret that Stone lived with, and despair, at how life can unfold, a despair that seemed to touch not only Stone and Celeste but me as well. In compensation for how Stone had rescued me I came to care for him, I knew that, for those moments of his kindness, a rescue from the uncertainty of being destitute, but also I saw now, of being without a family.

During my anxious pacing I did not consider Martin, with whom I had just shared an afternoon of lovemaking; instead I walked back and forth before the window, thinking about how I had ended up in that room and what kept me there. I had told Martin I had to return, said I was expected and besides we should not see each other all the time. "Too much of a good thing," I'd said, but it was more than that. I needed to come back here. It had become home, dysfunctional certainly, but a home, nevertheless. As I was wrestling with these thoughts, Stone knocked. "Melanie?" he said and opened the door.

"Stone, I'd like a lock on my door. I know Celeste said you don't like them, but I need my privacy." I was being contrary, for if I was honest, it was not my intention to stay at Winter Willow much longer.

He ignored me. "Where were you?"

"Besides there is a lock on the door leading to the third floor. So it's not every room."

He ignored me again. "I asked where you were."

"Out. Living my life."

"How can you answer me like that?" He was using a cane, something I had never seen before. Its handle was an elaborate head of a lion in bronze. "I'm asking for merely a little courtesy at this important moment."

"I'm here, aren't I, Stone? And I've been nothing if not courteous." This I knew to be untrue, but I had not been deliberately cruel either. "You don't want me to feel imprisoned here, do you?" And yet saying this the thought came to me that it was exactly how I felt, imprisoned, and I had to wonder by what. Stone's expectations? I suppose if I had been willing to admit it at the time, it was partly by my own naïve belief that I could manipulate the situation of that house to my benefit.

I sat on the bed, my back to him and he said before leaving, "I should be concentrating on my new novel, working on what I will say at the conference, but instead I spend my days thinking about you." How sadly he said those words. As far as I could tell, he had not written anything since we met, and I felt the house was crumbling under the weight of this failure. Winter, its sleepy permanence, filled the hallways, the rooms where we read or worked or ate in silence. It was a subterranean world, a world where our emotions were paralyzed by a suppression of memories and desires. I heard Stone descend the stairs and realized I knew very little about him. At least it seemed to me I knew very little that was true about him.

. . .

The next day as I'd promised myself I went to see Martin in his office. He stood when I entered, crossed the room, closed the door and without saying a word took both my wrists over my head and kissed me. The memory of our lovemaking made my body open to him. I didn't want him to stop, but he did, abruptly, and returned to his desk. "So, I've been thinking," he said.

"Oh no," I said, smiled, and approached him. "Are you sure that's a good idea?"

"Yeah," he grinned. "But no, listen. If you really focus you can finish your thesis by next term, or the one after that, and me too, I could finish by next summer."

"So, I don't see the world caring or clamoring to give us jobs."

"Why are you being so cynical?" I went closer still and when he stood I went to kiss him, but he moved his head back. "It's that place."

"What?" I moved away.

"Every time you come back, you're different. It takes you a while to get back to being yourself."

"How do you know who I am? How do you know when I'm being myself? I barely know. So how can you?"

We retreated to either side of the room, pacing, not looking at each other.

"You must know," he said after the silence had thickened between us. "How I feel. How I want to be with you. You're the only thing I care about. Not this place, not my life before you came." He was looking out the window as he spoke, his voice soft. What had he changed to be with me, I wondered. He had made his relationship with his wife seem like an arrangement made before they knew each other, something they both saw, not as a mistake, but as a stage they both were comfortable leaving.

"I love you too," I said.

"What I'm saying," he ignored what I said and walked toward me, "is we need to make plans to be together, we can't keep on like this." I knew he was speaking about my leaving Stone and Winter Willow.

"He won't like it," I said softly, as if to myself, looking away. It was snowing again. "I have to leave, Martin," I said, knowing Stone was expecting me and knowing too that I needed to be alone to think. Rather than debate me or question what I said, as I expected, he moved back to the window to view the courtyard below and did not move his glance or answer me. I left, knowing I'd disappointed him.

• • •

Walking in the cold, holding my scarf and collar close to my neck, I wondered how I'd ended up there, under a sky that seemed heavy with judgment. When I looked up, Elsa was before me, standing at the bus stop. She was speaking to a woman who was actively ignoring her, looking beyond Elsa's head to the road, anxious, I could tell, for the bus to appear. "Well, looky," Elsa said when she saw me. Her thin greying hair was in two high ponytails and I wondered when I saw her what delusion of style had prompted such a look. She was wearing her father's construction boots and her mother's fur coat over a chiffon dress.

"Elsa," I said, and the woman beside her looked toward me quizzically.

"Melly," she smiled so that I could see teeth missing at the side of her mouth. Had I missed noticing this before, or was it something new? "It fell through. I didn't have to move," she said, still grinning.

"What do you mean?"

"The sale fell through. I'm still in my same room." She was holding both my hands in her mittened hands. "There's a man living in your room. I don't like him much." She leaned closer to me and whispered, "He reminds me of the mailman."

"Really? You're still there."

"The owner said the deal fell through."

I missed Elsa. I missed hearing the simple way she had of viewing the world. "I need to get home right now," I freed one of my hands and patted the sleeve of her coat. "But I'll come to see you soon".

"I did try to contact you, you know, Melanie, but they told me you didn't live there. I thought maybe you could move back." Elsa then turned back to the woman who was still waiting for the bus but who now smiled at her. "She used to live in my rooming house," I heard Elsa say as I walked away.

As I started back along the street, I wondered if Stone was somehow responsible for the sale of the rooming house, if it had been his way of forcing me to move in with him and once I did then there was no need to go through with the sale. The farther I walked the truer it felt. Our initial meeting in the cold garden had awakened some need in Stone and I knew he could have easily arranged through Gavin to start the purchase of the rooming house. I walked toward Winter Willow with a new determination. And yet I knew that confronting Stone with my questions would most likely prove fruitless, for even if he revealed that he'd manipulated the situation, nothing could negate the months I'd spent at Winter Willow and what I'd learnt there.

I reasoned that my suspicion was with good cause, for it seemed that there were forces beyond my agency that controlled many elements in my life, and some of these forces, I now realized, were tied to Stone's will. The thought chilled me, just as the wind which picked up at that moment and blew my hair across my face, chilled me. But I kept my determined progress, leaning into the cold until I reached Winter Willow.

When I opened the door, I was greeted by the dense quiet of the house, its numbing silence. The library door was open, and I could see books on the floor where I had left them, a desk piled with papers, motionless, familiar as a stage. I let the view sink into me and felt its power to deaden. I wanted to destroy the room. It felt as if my salvation depended upon it. As I stood there Celeste came along the hallway from the back of the house. "Melanie. Stone was looking for you," she said. "But right now, he's in the upstairs library with Gavin."

"Good, I'd like to speak with both of them."

"Oh no, you can't disturb them."

Her face was clenched with worry, but I moved around her and mounted the stairs. I had not bothered to remove my coat or boots. On the second floor, the door to the library was closed and I entered without knocking. "I need to speak to you, Stone."

"I'm busy, as you can see," he said, his voice surprised, but growing annoyed.

"Actually, I have a question for the both of you." Gavin looked at me unsmiling. "Did you start the process to buy the house where I lived?" He raised his hand as if to say something but changed his mind and looked toward Stone. His deference to Stone told me my supposition was most likely true.

Stone said, "Melanie, please. Let me finish here." He came out from behind the desk, tried to walk toward me but had to stop and leaned against it. When had he become so pitifully frail? Then I remembered what the secretary in the English department had said about how everyone had noticed this frailness. How had I been so blind? "Something has upset you and I think we should talk alone," he said.

I knew I sounded like a petulant child, but this merely increased my anger. "Enough," I said, "enough of all these secrets and your manipulations". But I faltered then, could say no more. With both men quiet, watching me, I became unable to formulate my thoughts and I was concerned by the appearance of Stone, and so turned to leave them alone.

In my room I lay on the bed when thoughts of my mother came to me. I imagined her asking me what had I expected when I moved there. That Stone would save me? That I needed saving? I thought how for years her life was lived in the same routine, and how in the rare contemplative moments of her day—I knew, because I knew her so well—she would think of me and what my life was to become. It was her dearest wish that I succeed, as if I were the fragment of her that was the most precious. Now I wonder about the hours she spent at her work, how during this period in her life, I was inching my way toward the independence of leaving, while a cancer was growing inside her. I had not felt such grief about my mother for months, but there it was back again, stabbing in its intensity, and all I could do was wait for the moment to move on and be put in context of the day.

I heard Stone and Gavin in the hallway and later Gavin descend the stairs. Stone knocked at my door, "Melanie, please open up." He sounded reasonable, far more reasonable than I had sounded just a few moments earlier. I did not answer, and the door swung into the room, Stone in its opening. An old man with sinewy hands, one on the door handle, the other by his side on a cane, and with his grey hair growing out of its neat cut into something shaggy. I realized as I walked toward him that there had been a marked disintegration in his physical being, or perhaps I just had not noticed until this day how final it seemed. In any case, the sad decline revealed what had always been there, and that was that his privilege and self-aggrandizement had allowed a certain element of madness to infiltrate his thinking. It was a madness only revealed when you knew him, for he had learnt how to look a certain way and speak in a way so that you would think he was merely eccentric. I saw now, in the glint of his eye, the lean on his cane and the way he watched me, that he did not see the world the same way most people would, as existing beyond him with as much claim to truth or viability as his own existence.

The revelation stilled me. I was locked within his vision as an image and I could picture myself as he saw me: his captive, a young woman caught in her own need for recognition and unable to see what she represented to him. How had I avoided knowing this until this moment? The cuff of his sleeve was frayed and there were stains on his white shirt. I wondered if it was the hours of solitude spent in his library, when the night came in and he could not tell when the long continuous moments of thinking melded into the logic of sleep or a dream, when people from his past, his family, visited and became as real as those who shared his house. Days and nights when his way of being, of seeing his life, intermingled, so that upon waking he often grew unaware and confused about where he was. And always the firm guidance of Celeste, with her meals and routine. No doubt locked in her own uncertainties and assumptions. Why was this so clear now? With Stone standing at the door, watching me with renewed suspicion.

He could see in me some new dangerous knowledge forming, and his face slackened. "You think you can leave me, don't you?" he said.

"Yes, I do, and I will, soon."

"No, you will not leave, at least not until I do."

"I don't think so, Stone." My thoughts about him and his sad condition made me forget the resentment I felt about his likely buying the rooming house and left me feeling merely weary. He straightened; his eyes narrowed.

"No." He stepped into the room and I saw he was trembling—with anger or infirmity, I could not tell. But whatever it was made him incapable of speaking, until he said, "Oh, Catherine". He stumbled, looked past me, backed up, and after a moment's silence when he looked away, closed the door. Had I misheard? Had I really again called me Catherine, or was he just recalling her at that moment? The exchange awakened a drowsy awareness of him in the room with me, that he had called me by her name when he visited, but then perhaps I had imagined that too.

I had thought the sleepy, paralyzing hours of the past week came from the continuous fall of snow and the way the sun was blocked, so that the isolation we'd known was from an exterior source. But now I wondered if it hadn't been Stone, his character and will, that quieted the house and left a claustrophobic sense of being locked away.

I knew I had to leave and the sooner I did, the better, but when I reached the door it was locked from the outside. When had locks been installed? I knocked on the door, called for Stone, but heard nothing in response. After a few minutes I decided it made sense to wait for Stone or Celeste to return and to rest until they did. The room, its staid furniture, the curtains hanging limply, seemed to show time stilled to this moment of my entrapment.

* * *

A few hours later, as I lay quietly on the bed following the silence into a near sleep, the door opened and Celeste stood before me. "You shouldn't make him so angry."

"I shouldn't?"

Celeste was carrying a tray with food, and I noticed how bent she was and wondered if this deterioration was new, if it had struck the two of them at the same time. "Look Celeste, I don't belong here. You know that. You know it's time for me to leave. Just let me go."

"But he likes to have you here, Melanie. You remind him of something, maybe of when he was young." She placed the tray on the desk. "But you're too young to know how that would feel, how important it would be to be reminded of your youth."

As she spoke she walked backward to leave the room and did not shift her glance from me. I thought how she would never leave Stone, never willingly anyway. "Just let me go," I stood, walked toward her.

"You can, at any time."

"But the door was locked."

"These doors can't lock. You know that."

And she was right, when I examined the door it did not have a latch that locked. "But I couldn't open it, after Stone left."

"I do not understand you, Melanie," she said. "Can you not see how ill he is? Do you not care at all?" I did not answer, and she closed the door with a neat click. I was alone once again, staring at the space she'd just occupied. I looked at the tray, fish and rice, and imagined her earlier that day, cooking this food, scurrying about the kitchen, frantic in her subservience, following a routine so ingrained that she had barely to think about it. And what did she think about? What past continued to haunt her? No doubt it was her life with Stone, the years she spent at Winter Willow, first with him, his mother and second wife and then with his third wife. Always the supplicant. And now as she aged, it seemed as if there was an urgency to her desire to protect him, to commemorate the sacrifice her life had been in service to him.

The house was hugely quiet, like a river on a calm, sun-drenched day, a river that had smoothed to reflect evenly the sky and trees on a distant shore, but where a current ran below the surface with a muscular strength.

Tomorrow I will leave, I will begin my life with Martin. No doubt we will make mistakes and have regrets, but we will create memories and move on into the years and all will settle as it was meant to. I ate in silence the last meal Celeste would make for me.

# 18

I woke early the next morning with the thought I wanted to see my old rooming house and as I knew Elsa was an early riser, I decided to walk there. Stone and Celeste were not awake when I left. The sky was clear, a calm Wedgewood blue, unmarked by clouds, the sunlight candy-hard on the streets, the trees, the shiny mounds of snow pushed off sidewalks. Despite the sterile cold, there was a sense of spring in the air, a promise of its return.

Visiting Elsa would be a way to visit my recent past. Seeing her, seeing the vestibule with its metal mail slots, the dreary crowded hallways submerged in the gloomy light from the overhead lamp, was a way to balance what had passed with what would come. I was a different person from the woman who had lived there, whose life was spent in quiet pursuits—reading, writing, thinking about London in the early twentieth century. When I stopped in front the house and looked at its brooding mass, the word 'home' came to mind, but then, 'no longer', as I walked toward the entrance. Eve was coming out the front door, carrying her bike.

"Melanie," she said surprised. "Are you moving back?"

"Oh no, just visiting Elsa."

"Too bad you left before the sale fell through. You're the only person who did."

"I thought you had decided to leave too," I said.

"I had, but then it just made more sense to stay here when it turned out the house wasn't going to be sold."

She put down her bike on the snow-packed path. "I can't believe you've used your bike all winter," I said. "There's been some awful storms."

"But only a few days when I really couldn't use it." She swung her leg around the bike. "She's in there, I saw her this morning," she said before carefully moving off.

When I buzzed Elsa, she opened the door to her apartment and came to the vestibule, looking through the small rectangular window. Her face brightened when she saw it was me. "Oh, you said you'd come, but I didn't know it'd be so soon. How lovely." She was already dressed for the day, in an emerald-coloured quilted vest over an embroidered shirt, with a taffeta skirt that made a majestic sound as she moved.

On her feet she wore only heavy socks and when I noticed I said, "Elsa, you'll catch your death. Put some shoes on."

"Come in, come in," she said, still smiling and busying herself making tea which she knew I'd want. The large rose-coloured chair that had been my mother's was in the middle of her room. I sat on it and to her back said, "Elsa, do you know who tried to buy the rooming house?"

"No. It was a bit of a mystery." She turned to look at me after putting water in the kettle. "Some property company, I think. Why, Melanie? Why do you want to know?"

"Oh, it really doesn't matter at this point," I said. "I just wanted to see you. I've missed you."

"That's nice," She sat on one of the kitchen chairs by the counter. "I've missed you too." Her living space—as my own had been—was one large area, the sections delineated by furniture. She began to speak of the new tenant in my old room, how messy he was and unfriendly, and as she did I remembered the person I had been only months earlier, when I lived beside her. I felt a strange nostalgia for that woman, for it seemed I'd lost something crucial that had allowed me to be her—the student, the daughter, Elsa's friend. The crowded space of the apartment where I sat was so different from the dusty and voluminous spaces of Winter Willow that I quietly looked around and barely spoke as I listened to Elsa's complaints.

After our tea and talk, while I was putting on my coat, winding the scarf around my neck, she said, "How do you find living in that neighbourhood?" She was tidying the counters and putting the cups in the sink. "I know I hated it there."

"What? You've lived in that neighbourhood?"

"I grew up on that street. Not far from the house where you're staying."

"I had no idea Elsa."

"But didn't I tell you? I thought I had. My brother still lives in my old house."

"Did you know the family who lived at Winter Willow?"

"I knew Sonia, she was a couple of years older than me." Sonia, I knew from Celeste, was Stone's sister.

"And Stone, did you know him?"

"He was away. In the war, I heard. And when he came back we seldom saw him." Elsa had turned from the counter and was close to me so that we were eye to eye as she spoke.

"What was he like? Then?"

"Stone? Well, all I remember was at Sonia's funeral, he was broken, and his mother too. They looked like broken teacups sitting in the pew, pieced together but you know, broken just the same."

"Yes, I heard it was hard on them."

"After Sonia died, that's when I decided to leave my house. I hated all those large rooms and long hallways." She backed up to sit on the straight chair once again and I noticed how stiff she had become, that she rubbed her right thigh. "You see she was my friend, my only friend there, and I didn't want to end up like her, so I told my family I was leaving."

She wasn't looking at me as she spoke, and I could tell she was thinking back on those days. "I like it so much better here. Here you can hold your home close, see it all at once."

"You are so right Elsa," I said turning the door handle. "And thank you for the tea, and our talk. I'll come back soon."

She brightened. "Please do. Spring is coming, it will be easier for you. In fact it will be easier for everyone then."

•  •  •

Sorrow rules life, I thought as I walked the familiar streets back to Winter Willow. Sorrow and joy intermingled certainly, the dark known by the light, but it is sorrow, attached as it is to loss, that stays lodged in the mind and heart, more steadfast, more insistent, more intrusive, especially as you grow older.

•  •  •

When I returned to Winter Willow, it was with the conviction I would leave shortly. It was still early in the day and in my room I gathered my possessions, placed clothes in a suitcase, books in boxes, as the struggling sun stretched into the room where I worked; it seemed to reach out to me, to placate and soothe. I did not see Celeste all day. When I went to the kitchen to eat, I saw a light under the door that led to her suite of rooms. Sitting at the table, having cereal, I looked out to the garden where the snow was starting its slow melt.

•  •  •

Because the temperature was slightly warmer than it had been for the past few weeks, when I went back in my room, I wanted to let some fresh air into the space, so I opened the wooden framed window. It took a forceful tug to release it from its closed winter position. A loud creak issued when it jerked up and when I glanced down I saw that Stone was below in the garden. The sound startled him so that he looked up, his hand shielding his eyes, and when he saw me, he gestured for me to come down. I wanted to continue my packing, but instead I descended the stairs, grabbed my jacket, scarf and slipped on the boots I kept on the back veranda. I opened the door to the garden.

"Do you remember, my dear, the first time we met was here?" he said when I joined him.

"Of course," I said, wrapping the scarf around my neck, but keeping my jacket open. "I came here feeling quite destitute."

He made a grunt as if to say he remembered. "My mother planted most of this garden." He walked ahead of me slowly down the central path as I followed, but then turned abruptly, "Melanie, have you seen my cane? That cane that had been my father's?"

"No, Stone. When did you lose it?"

"I couldn't find it this morning. This one was in the main hall," he said, moving the cane in his hand through the air before him. "But I don't like it nearly as much." He turned from me and continued along the path, head bent, his pace steady but slow.

After a few moments he said, "This was my mother's garden. She planned the colours, the way there would always be something in bloom."

When I caught up to him, I said, "I'm sure it must be wonderful in the spring and summer."

"And now, look how this garden has survived and yet she's been gone for so many years." He put both hands on his cane and looked around at the muddle of bent plants just beginning to emerge from under the mounds of snow. "She used to say people had it all wrong about winter being a time of hibernation. It's really a time of reckoning, of seeing where life has brought you."

I was watching him closely, the way he squinted into the sun, the way his speech slowed, and his walking was stilted and awkward. "Reckoning?" I said.

"Yes, this garden has survived storms, winds, blazing heat, and it has also had temperate, lovely weather, soft spring rains, or the early evening cooling in autumn."

What is he trying to tell me, I wondered as I took his arm so that he could lean on me as he walked.

"And through it all, like something programmed in the garden itself, in its very foundation, the idea that every spring some of these plants will not bloom."

He stopped walking and I stopped beside him: a young woman, an old man. The canopy of sky was strewn with clouds, the otherworldly light fell along the passageway where we stood. We were encircled by the dormant beds of dogwood, hydrangeas, lavender, prickly roses, peonies, lilies, all lying still under a covering of dense snow.

"Stone," I said. "The wind is picking up. We should go in."

"Yes, yes, you're right. I need to rest."

Slowly we made our way to the back porch, mounted the steps and went through the veranda to the kitchen where Stone said, "I'll see you later Melanie. I need to speak with Celeste." I left him there knocking on her door and would never know if she answered.

# 19

There was a phone in the main hallway on the wall outside the vestibule, which I had noticed but had never seen anyone use before, until that night, when I heard Stone speaking on it. I moved to the top of the staircase to better hear, but still his voice was not clear, so I went to the top of the steps, sat down and listened.

"She's upstairs," I heard him say. "I just want to make sure the changes I made a few weeks ago, that there were no problems, that they're on record. Do you understand, Gavin?" Stone was holding the phone with one hand, leaning on his cane with the other. I could not hear what Gavin said, but after a few moments of Stone listening, I heard, "Well, I don't care. It's my wish. My last wish." Then he hung up and turned around. He saw me sitting far up on the steps. What a sad, foolish man he looked, with his surprise and simple fumbling and I wondered then how I could have been so intimidated by him when we first met.

"What are you scheming?" I said. "What are your plans now with Gavin?"

I could see by the way he looked away, sighed, that a weariness had overtaken him, and he dropped to the chair kept by the door. We both sat like this for a few moments, he looking down at the floor and me staring mildly at him.

I said, "Did you really think you could keep me here?"

But he did not answer, instead he massaged his chest and after a few moments looked up toward me, then shifted his gaze down the hall, his expression freshly alert as if he saw someone there. "No, I agree this cannot continue. Will you please come down here, Melanie, in a few minutes, after I do something I must do first. We need to speak."

A sudden feeling of calm filled me, and I remained seated on the top of the stairs listening to the stately quiet of the house. Where was Celeste I wondered when, after ten minutes, I moved down the stairs to follow him to the library. The calmness I felt made me able to forgive him, for it seemed I was always able to forgive him, and wasn't this, I wondered then, in the final analysis, also evidence of love.

In the library he was standing by the window. I shut the door and he moved to behind the desk. "I'm dying," he said. "You must have sensed that."

The admission, so far from anything I imagined he'd say, shocked but I said calmly. "Yes." And when I said it I knew it was true, the word I had not let myself think, but yes, I did believe I'd been watching him die. "I've noticed you've been failing, Stone."

"No, not failing, I am dying now. Right now. Before you."

After saying this and his glance shifting toward the window, he sat down slowly in the chair behind his desk, succumbing to an old tiredness. With his admission an increased calmness filled me. I sat quiet until he said, "I'm looking forward to it, to escaping." I could see his pale eyes, filmed and dull. "That's the thing you don't know, won't know for many years, how the idea of death can be a relief, how much sense it makes." No longer was he angry or animated or for that matter willful. He was merely old, and I was sure now, a man welcoming the idea of death. It was as if the space had filled with grey water, holding me in place, weighing both of us on either side of the room, locked in the moment. I will escape this room, I thought. And he will not. Even in witnessing this, his final struggle, it will be me who endures, my youth and energy vindicated. I will inherit what is left by Stone, what has been left by his generation, and it will be a victory of sorts. His death I knew was meant to scar what was young and impressionable in me, so that I would keep its continually altering shape with me as it grew in insistence during the years to come. And yet as I watched him, a raw and heartless stillness settled in me, making me feel expansive, and as he grew less prominent, an urge to laugh overtook me. But I kept it at bay with my desire to observe unfettered by emotions.

His hands were under the desk and I saw him grimace—with pain, I wondered—and then I saw his head fall slightly backward. His eyes closed. Could he be having a heart attack? And yet his movements were so slight it seemed unlikely. I came closer, closer still and when he did not move, I knew he was unconscious or close to unconsciousness. What am I witnessing, I wondered, for I could feel a shift between us, a transferring of power, when I felt I could rise omnipotent over the scene. I heard a sound like a gurgle, and then a moan, unrushed and faint. He opened his filmed eyes and looked at me, said her name, "Catherine". I didn't correct him. I was to be the last image he'd see, and I wonder, all these years later, if it was kindness or weariness that made me stand there uncomprehending and smile down at him one last time.

There it was, an empty bottle of pills mixed in with the papers and clutter of his desk. Of course, I thought, he'd taken medication after speaking to Gavin, pills that would kill him. The realization was replaced by an urgency to relinquish the moment to others, to those who could help change the act into tasks to be performed, involving ambulances, hospitals, the outside world.

But before others would join us, I remained for one reckless moment to register this dying man, this man who chose to use his last shred of concentrated will to end the long, complex, weary trail he had made through life. Was it strength or cowardice? I'd never know. All these thoughts crowded in when I heard the door open behind me and Celeste enter the room. "What have you done?" she said carefully, quietly. It was a good question and it stuck between us as she moved closer, her hand now at her mouth, an anguish radiating from her like light.

"Call an ambulance," I said, landing us both back in that place where things needed to be done.

• • •

The paramedics arrived quickly, followed by police and other people I could not identify. I went to the living room, or salon as Stone had always called it, a room that went usually unused and where the party had taken place mere weeks before, and heard the commotion of people arriving, shouting to each other, their loud stomping in hallways. We flung the sheets off the furniture, placed there for protection. Celeste was with me, sitting in a straight back chair against the wall. Initially she was rocking and muttering, what she said I could not make out, except for the soft chant of, *no, not Stone, not Stone.* Then she became quiet and stared ahead as if she could hear sounds I could not. I sat in a loveseat watching her, asking questions she would not answer. "Did you know he would do this?" "How did he behave this afternoon?" "Did he say anything to you?"

A police officer, one of the people who was in the first group to arrive, entered the room. His expressionless face gave off an air of boredom as he looked at Celeste and then turned to me, "So, you were with him?" he said.

"Yes," I said. "He was speaking, rambling actually. I couldn't understand."

"Why didn't you stop him?" Celeste said, shifted her view from in front of her to me. She was now alert and her question was pointed with derision. Why, indeed? Because this was how it was meant to be, I thought. I felt a dull resentment as I looked at her and saw an old woman, her mind tattered, her face crumpled. How foolish you are, I thought, watching her, sure that the policeman could not see my face, but that she could. Her expression faded quickly, and she again went back to rocking and muttering.

"What's wrong with her?" the policeman asked.

"Upset. They were very close." But of course it was more than that. I knew that something central to Celeste's view of the world was gone, something that would never be replaced.

"And who are you? I mean to him?"

"I work and live here." I was about to tell him how long I'd lived at Winter Willow but then thought, could it have been less than three months? "He has died, hasn't he?" I asked as he continued writing in a notepad.

"Yes, he's dead," he said absently, without looking up. Celeste made a sobbing sound and he said, looking at me, "Well, she understood that." He stood, walked toward her and said, "I'm going to have a paramedic look at you." Then to me, "I think she's in shock."

Before he left the room to get the paramedics, he turned and said, "By the way, he had a knife in his hand. Did you see that?"

"No. No. He just seemed to fall away."

Two paramedics came into the room, crouched to speak with Celeste and after asking a few unanswered questions, decided she should be taken to the hospital. They held her elbows and guided her from the room. Watching her leave, I thought she looked old in a new way.

The policeman continued. "This guy, he was a writer, wasn't he?"

"Yes, yes, he was," I said and remembered I still had not reread his novel, that was on my bedside table upstairs, waiting for me. A few weeks later when I picked up the book to pack, I noticed the inscription from Stone on the title page, *To Melanie, with the hope of all good things, and with my love, old and weary as it is.*

. . .

After Celeste and the crowd of people who had descended on Winter Willow were gone, taking with them the noise and activity that had ricocheted throughout the rooms of the house, and after Stone's body had been removed, I was alone there for the first time. Often I'd been alone in my room, but then there was always the sense of Stone and Celeste close by, and the sense too that they were monitoring me, so that I had not felt free to roam about the house. Being here after everyone had left, after having seen Stone's death and Celeste's break from reality, I thought of how heartless my survival seemed, that somehow that I was the person left standing seemed a surprise and somehow fundamentally unfair.

I walked to the kitchen where I could see the garden stretching into the dark and turned on the back lamps. It was once again snowing, one of the last storms of the season, so that light filtered through the flakes, filling the garden with time, illuminating the snow-laden bushes and dips of the pathways.

I found in the snow's graceful fall a logic or meaning missed in all my pointed thoughts of Celeste and Stone. I heard the phone's echoed ring—the inspector calling, asking if I would be there the next day so that he could return to ask more questions.

After I hung up, and before I could move away, it rang again. I thought the inspector had forgotten to tell me something, so I answered quickly, 'yes' and Martin said, "Melanie, is it true?"

"How do you know?"

"Some students were on the street, saw the ambulance and police. Is it true?"

"That Stone is dead. Yes."

"I'm coming over." But I told him I was still answering questions and didn't know when I'd be free. When I hung up I was glad I'd lied, but I knew that doing so marked me as a certain type of person. For the sensation of being alone in that large house—a house I realized standing by the back door that I had not explored, that still had a third floor that was a mystery—filled me with a powerful, new-found sense of freedom.

## 20

In one of the lower kitchen cabinets I had seen a ring on a hook with an assortment of keys, and when I'd seen it I thought the door key to the third floor was most likely there. And so, remembering this ring with a sudden urgency, I retrieved it and mounted the staircase to the second floor. In the hallway I noticed Stone's bedroom door had been opened and wondered who had done that. The coroner? The police? I stopped. The room remained static and stately and I felt something like regret that after this day it would never again have Stone within its walls. It was my first real pang of grief for him.

It took a few tries of different keys until I found the one that would unlock the door leading to the third floor, and when I did and pushed the door open, the hinges creaked. I turned on the light. There was a staircase with a landing and window looking out to the side yard, a small bank of snow on the sill outside. At the top of the staircase was a short hallway that led to an open area, cluttered with furniture and boxes, an old easel with a dusty half-finished canvas. I remembered that Celeste had told me Stone's third wife had been an artist. The image on the canvas was of a man prone on a settee. He was naked, and I wondered if that could have been Stone in the 1950s, the decade I was born. I opened a large armoire and saw what must have been Stone's military uniforms and medals. What will become of these, I wondered. It was as if his life, its many versions and stages were all laid out here, dusty under the bald glare thrown from the dangling light bulb. That he had been living just that morning, that I had seen him, spoken to him, struck me now with a sense that his essence was still here, and that it was his will that was showing me these things that would survive him.

Off in the corner, draped in shadow, was another armoire, the door of it open. I could see clothes hanging in it, and on the bottom shelf boots and shoes. The clothes were mostly men's clothes from another era, there were long raincoats, suit jackets, fedoras on the top shelf, clothes I imagined Stone had worn years before. When I closed the door I noticed beside it there was a small table, with candles in holders, and what looked like papers scattered around them. It was dark and my sight was adjusting slowly, so that I was able to make out about a dozen or so candles of varying heights—some in a candelabra, some which had never been lit, others burnt almost to the quick. I saw matches and lit one of the candles to better see what was on the table. In the silky dark, the candlelight flickered.

In the middle of the table was a large photograph in a silver filigreed frame. It showed the face of a woman, and as I moved the candle closer to better see, I was shocked. I sat down in the straight back chair before the desk and stared, for the face in this large photograph in the middle of all this disarray, was of my mother. How could this be? But then I moved the candle closer still and realized that although the resemblance was striking, it was not her. And I knew without being told, or without having it confirmed in any way, that this was the face of Catherine.

Scattered around this central photograph were other papers and photos. I put the candle holder down in order to look through them. Some were of Stone and his mother and sister, many I recognized from the framed photos he had around the house. But there were a few at the bottom of the stack of Stone and Catherine. I knew this because when I flipped the first one over their names and the date were clearly marked with the notation, 'our wedding day'. Catherine wore what looked like a velvet cape with white fur trim, her long blonde hair in loose curls. They were both smiling, both aflame with something like promise. That she looked like my mother meant, I knew, that she also looked like me. Not exactly, of course, but enough to give pause, for someone to stop and think us related if they saw us together. The photographs of Stone and Catherine were black and white, so I could not tell her eye colour, but she looked happy and young, and I had pictured her, when Celeste had told me stories or when Stone mentioned her, as neither of these things.

When I looked closer I could see she was wearing under the cape the dress Stone had given me, so here was proof he'd bought it before the end of the war. Once again I wondered about my role in this, the last stage of Stone's life. Then I thought, *let it go.* Let it go and be grateful if my presence gave him comfort, for comfort is one of the few things, in the final analysis, we can give each other.

In the next photograph they were sitting at a table in what appeared to be a café. Stone's hair was thick, wavy and dark, and he was leaning over the table in earnest conversation with another man. The image captured Stone's animation and good humour, and something too of how handsome he was. Catherine beside him was smiling, her hair in thick waves around her face and there seemed a festive air about the scene.

I put my hand beside me on the chair and felt the cane that Stone had complained of losing. The lion's head handle was bumpy under my hand and I thought, so this was what he was doing when I heard him above me during all those evenings. He was sitting here, exactly in this spot, looking at these remnants of his life with Catherine.

I sat at the desk for a few more minutes, contemplating the man in those images, the man so young I could barely recognize him as the same person I'd watch die earlier that night. That I was the person left to discover these lost mementoes from his past, seemed such an improbability that I was silenced and a little awed by the capricious-ness of the moment that found me alone in that attic.

Yet what had I expected to find there, the answer to the mystery of Stone? Because he was and would remain a mystery, one that could not be explained by his possessions, which now seemed bereft of meaning, or by his house with its massive rooms and furnishings and its impressive garden. My rummaging through those private objects was an attempt to understand him, surely, but it was also in effect an attempt to reduce him to an entity that could be understood. And yet I knew this quest would not give me the answers I sought. It would not explain Stone and his past, the authority of war, and how these things were able to influence his character. The space merely housed the remnants of a life, a full life, that saw war and love and witnessed how each could be entrapped, entangled, and finally enlarged into a form of art.

• • •

Returning to the kitchen and the view of the garden, I opened a bottle of wine and poured a glass. I put the photographs of Stone and Catherine on the counter. So this had been Stone then, at my age, locked in these fading images and lost in a pile of photographs. I could see my reflection in the pane of the window looking out to the snow-laden bushes and trees. It reminded me of the night before my mother died when I was with her at the hospital and I stood by the window looking down to the hospital's parking lot. I could see the red-lit sign for the Emergency entrance obscured by a snowstorm.

I'd gone to the cafeteria to get a coffee and when I returned, I saw Mr. Mendelson, my mother's employer, in the hallway, having just left her room. He was somber and when I stood before him his eyes lit on me. "Melanie," he said with sadness.

"Mr. Mendelson," I answered. "Have you been to see my mother?" I was shocked to see him there, in the hallway, to see his grim expression and know that the sight of my mother had caused the grief I was witnessing.

"Yes, yes," he said. We stopped before each other and while I watched him, he looked away, toward the large window at the end of the hall. "She's..." he faltered, put his hand up to his face. "She's leaving us, isn't she?" But before I could answer he said, "I'm so sorry, so very sorry."

It had probably been a decade since I'd seen him, since that day I interrupted my mother and him in her office. He looked frailer than I remembered, and there was none of the good humour in his attitude that I had seen that day.

"Thank you for coming to see her," I said. "I hope she was awake."

"Yes, she opened her eyes, said my name." He looked directly at me after saying this, so that what I was going to say—something about how it was a good thing my mother was awake, as she was often sleeping—was forgotten and I remained quiet. "This is so wrong. This is not what should have happened," he said, once again looking away from me.

"I agree," was all I was able to say before he walked past me and slowly left me standing there alone in the hallway.

. . .

In my mother's room, I returned to the chair placed beside her bed for me by one of the orderlies. She was awake but not looking at me and did not speak for a few minutes. "You were the only real thing in my life, Melanie. You were the only promise of something better than what I had." She turned toward me then, her eyes glistening and in a breaking voice said, "Because you see, we all live lives of the heart." She paused to swallow, "And sometimes the heart misguides." Her eyes lost their focus and she softly fell into a sleep. The sound of the room followed the rhythmic pattern of her deep breathing.

Sitting beside her as she slept, I thought how there must have been more to her relationship with Mr. Mendelson than merely employer, employee. She probably loved him, and this love had stalled her. I thought back to those countless mornings when she would be preparing for the day, fixing her hair, applying makeup, making lunches for the two of us, I thought about how while she did this the thought of him would have surfaced in her mind and had the power to overshadow everything else.

. . .

When I woke in the night, I saw that she was drifting awake.

"Listen Melanie," she said in a low voice when she realized I too was awake. "Listen to me, you're going to have to make it on your own now."

"Stop Mom. Stop speaking like this."

"No. You are." She closed her eyes, swallowed, and I knew she was having difficulty keeping her thoughts clear. "And I worry because sometimes you have an inability to take other people into account." On the pillow, her blonde hair streaked with grey lay in a chaotic mass around her face which looked swollen and drained pink, tinged with a yellow sheen, the eyebrows, light and willowy as wheat.

"You know, you amazed me at times." Her eyes still closed, she asked for ice chips, which the nurse had left in a styrofoam cup on the bedside table. I spooned the chips into her mouth. She lay still for a few moments until she said, "I know it will serve you well though. I know I can leave you alone and you'll be okay."

"I don't know what you're trying to say, Mother."

"With me gone," she said, "no one will really know you. Not truly." I watched her, the smooth skin of her quieting face, the heavy silence that held her, which extended from her body, to the room, even into the darkening evening.

Her body under the sheets was as small as a child, and the faded freckles across her nose gave her an elfin appearance.

The next day she fell into a coma, her breathing laboured. I sat beside her, watching all day. Nurses stopped by, patted my arm and I'd smile up at them. That day, near dusk, when the sky gleamed an unreal colour, she died with one final slow breath.

## 21

The next day, as promised, the police inspector came to the house where I had slept alone for the first time. Sitting at the kitchen table, he said the coroner's report was not ready yet, but it looked to him as if the conclusion would be suicide by pills. "It's unusual though," he said. "For a man his age."

"What do you mean?" I said.

"I mean, usually a man in his eighties does not kill himself." He stayed still after this statement and looked at me over his glasses. The silence lengthened between us.

"If you're asking me," I said, "if there were any indication he'd do this, I'd say no, but then he was increasingly frail, and maybe he knew he'd die soon and wished to avoid the pain."

"Yes, that seems logical," he bent his head while writing in a note-book. "But," he said, looking up again.

"But, what?" I said when he did not finish his sentence.

"But there's something you learn in this job, and that is people will take whatever kind of life they are given. So even if you think you'd kill yourself to avoid pain, when it comes to the actual moment, you probably wouldn't."

"Do you think I had something to do with Stone's death?" The thought cascaded over me with a chill.

"I don't know how you could," he said and asked again to see the room where Stone had died. On our way there, he said, "I have to consider it, you know. He changed his will less than a month ago. That's a red flag."

"I didn't want anything from Stone," I said, and once I heard those words I knew them to be untrue.

"Well, you're right that he was looking at a prolonged period of pain. I spoke to his doctor just before coming here."

"Stone's doctor?" I said. "I never saw him go to a doctor, or saw one come here."

"Shackelford was under his care for years. He'd come here just yesterday morning. He told me Shackelford would have been dead before the end of spring anyway."

More secrets. Good, I thought, that Stone had a life I did not know. Good for him.

After the policeman was gone, I wondered what Stone had left me and then what my role in his death had been. I was the last new person he came to know, and the last person he saw as he slipped out of his life, and surely, I thought, that must make me a crucial character in his personal drama, someone who certainly should know more than I did.

. . .

This all happened in the winter of the year 1976, the year I lost my university funding and put my PhD on hold, only to go back and finish the degree a year later. It was also the year I inherited Winter Willow and sold it to a corporation that turned it into an upscale restaurant, the year I discovered the wonder and confusion of being in love, and the year when I met and came to know Stone.

. . .

For special birthdays and events, during her young life, I would bring my daughter to the restaurant that was housed in the building I knew as Winter Willow. She is Martin's daughter, named Mary Jane, Janey for short, and she inherited his thick curly hair, its honey blonde colour, and his height. I would tell her during these meals about my experiences at Winter Willow, how I had known Stone, the writer whom the restaurant was named after. The stories bored her when she was young, but she returned to them as she became older and began to study literature herself. She would ask me to clarify what living with him had been like and what living in the 1970s generally had been like, as this was the era of Canadian literature she was studying.

When I'd go to the restaurant for a meal, it was difficult to remember how Winter Willow was when I lived there. A large dining room had replaced the segmented rooms on the second floor where my room and Stone's had been. In this way, by keeping Winter Willow part of the tradition of my family, going there to celebrate milestones, the building has stayed in my life, from that first day when I entered it with Stone from the garden, which in summer months now has a patio restaurant.

. . .

The third floor had been transformed into a piano bar, where jazz played on Friday evenings and where, for the first time, I saw Martin with the woman who would become his third wife. I had joined a group of colleagues who had decided to take in the music performed there. I did not know that some of these co-workers knew of Martin and this woman's affair and had thought it was high time I did also. She had been his student, and I could tell by the way she leaned over the table, the light from the candle making her seem even younger, her skin pink and plump, her eyelashes thick, their shadow spiked on her upper lid, that she was attentive in a way I could never be, even when we first met. Watching them my first sad thought was to wonder what Martin was chasing now, what need had made him seek out this woman, this room, with its music providing a discordant backdrop. As I watched them, he moved hair from her eyes and spoke in that soft, humorous way I knew so well.

. . .

The period when I lived with Stone dulled in my memory for many years, those years occupied with the completion of my PhD, then the birth of my daughter, with the breakdown of my marriage, and the years after when I lived with only Janey, mirroring my own experience as a young girl. It is only now, when I can see the way one step in a life leads inexorably to the next, that I am drawn back to Winter Willow as it had been so many years ago, to its yawning, dusty, silent spaces—drawn back with gratitude and a touch of wonder for that young woman I had been. I would like to interrupt her as she read in the elaborate bedroom during a snowstorm, but like my students and even my daughter, my former self would see my intrusion as an annoyance, an interference, something best ignored.

. . .

There will always be a moment when your life turns back upon itself, when who you were, the places where you lived, the things you've done and thought, become more real than the moment you are occupying. You'll see with clarity the twists in the road that led to where you are, the accumulation of days spent in the rooms of your various homes, in schools, or on streets and buses. You'll remember mornings of thin blue light that fell on dressers, curtains, walls, the open door before the shadowed hallway, and evenings that descended in those rooms, settled in the surrounding yards with the same gravity and mystery as they settled in the rooms of foreign houses, the remote fields of other continents. The time I look back on, the pivot upon which my life, I now realize, seemed to turn, was when I was living at Winter Willow with Stone and Celeste, lost and grieving my mother's death with a sorrow I still feel at times these many years later. I did not know how that season would coil inside me, forgotten for decades but destined to return and bring with it the sense of continuity between my life then and my life now. When I'd go for a meal at Winter Willow, I'd pass through the door that Stone's mother had designed and see the light caught in the diamond shaped crystals. It would bring to mind the way they'd greeted me each time I entered that vestibule. And the smudged spectrum behind Stone's head that first day he showed me the beautiful glass design of the door.

. . .

After I sold Winter Willow, I bought a much smaller house in Rosemount Hill, near the rooming house where I had lived as a student. It was here Martin and I lived, and where I raised our daughter after he moved back to the States. And it was here during the summer of 1997, when my daughter was eighteen and decided she wanted to live in the United States with her father and the children from his third marriage, that I spent a summer alone. For the first time in years, I was not teaching a summer course, and the months lay out before me as an ocean of time.

My heart was bruised by the absence of my daughter and the house itself seemed emptied of life or meaning. Nothing hurt as badly as her leaving, not even the separation with Martin, especially since she was leaving as a way of rejecting me and the life I had made for the two of us. That thought stung deeply.

It was here, during this summer of living alone, that I began to think of Stone in earnest. I reread two of his novels and saw nothing of the man I'd known in them. In fact they were marked by a formal style that seemed stilted and from a different era, which of course they were. The summer was particularly hot and brilliant, and often by mid-day a strong sun would fall over the yard where I sat to read. By the time I'd retreat back to the house in late afternoon, my eyes would be bleary and take a while to adjust to the darkened rooms.

. . .

Near the end of that summer Joni visited, staying for three days. Over the years we had stayed in touch, mostly by letters, but there had also been visits to each other's homes and she had asked me to be the godmother of her fourth child, a daughter, a year younger than Janey.

I heard the phone ring from the yard where I was reading. "I need a break," Joni said as a greeting when I answered, out of breath.

"What do you mean?"

"I need to get away for a few days." Joni knew from the last letter I wrote her that I was alone, and I knew she was saying she needed to visit because my letter had a sad tone and she thought she could help.

"Come. Anytime. You know that."

◆  ◆  ◆

A week later, sitting on the deck in my backyard, sharing a bottle of pinot gris as the night came in slowly, she said "Kids. They hurt sometimes, don't they? It's like a love affair, but one where the other person never feels as strongly as you do."

"You're right," I said. "You'd never take from a husband what you take from a kid."

Joni had stayed married since she was nineteen and credited the relationship's success to having completely separate working spheres— she at a credit co-operative in the small town close to where they lived, and her husband at the farm they owned. "The less you see of each other, the better." But I knew their union was a formidable one, that it had survived the loss of one of their boys to a car accident when he was seventeen and years of financial insecurity.

Later in the evening, as the temperature cooled, I asked about her sister Angie.

"She's well, wellish, anyway. She's on her fourth husband and lives in Florida."

"Why does that seem so fitting, that Angie would end up in Florida?"

"Because it's easy to see her there. Doing her nails in the sun, lounging in a deck chair."

"You're right." I stood, yawned and went in the house, brought us both back sweaters.

"And you, my dear, what have you been doing this summer?" Joni said.

"It's strange, I've been thinking about Winter Willow. Do you remember I lived there with the writer Stone Shackelford? That's when I met Martin."

"Yes, I remember having to contact you at the university. When I called the rooming house no one could tell me where you went." I remembered then receiving a message from her, but in the midst of that winter with its power to paralyze, I had not answered her.

"Elsa knew, and Eve too, but no one else."

"Elsa, now there was a card."

"I loved Elsa, and I think a lot of people did," I said. "You should have seen her funeral. Her brother paid for it and the chapel was overflowing. It amazed me the people she had touched." And it was true, the eulogies took hours. I even spoke for a few moments, told the people gathered there how I had come to depend on her friendship and kindness. After the service her brother approached me about the chair I had given her.

"My sister said she wanted you to have that chair she refused to get rid of," he said without preamble.

"It had been mine, at one point," I said.

He made a dismissive sound, almost a snort. "Well actually she said it was to go to Janey, that's your daughter, isn't it?" And it did go to Janey, so that as Joni and I drank our wine as the night cooled the yard where we sat, that chair was sitting like a lumbering animal in my daughter's room, the room she had abandoned.

• • •

"Why are you thinking of that time so long ago anyway?" Joni folded her arms to ward off the chill.

"I see now how important it was in what happened in my life, that's all."

"I remember how happy you were that summer, and then in the autumn when you married Martin. That was a good time in your life."

◆ ◆ ◆

That night, falling asleep I too remembered the months after my move from Winter Willow when life became simpler, when Martin and I began living together, and the sale of Winter Willow allowed us to buy our home, the house where I still lived.

◆ ◆ ◆

In the autumn my daughter returned. She had decided she wanted to study in Canada and although she did not say it, I knew that she had missed me. Classes began in September, and the days became cooler and were taken up with more serious pursuits than my summer of reading. But, like the season at Winter Willow, I came to see that hot, sunny summer as yet another span of time that defined who I would become. I saw the arc of those weeks when most days had a similar routine, when I was alone and uninfluenced by obligation, as a bridge to the next stage of my life. In retrospect I see that that summer provided the same type of isolated span of time that my months at Winter Willow had given me.

◆ ◆ ◆

I still teach Virginia Woolf's *Mrs. Dalloway* in my twentieth-century literature class, as I have for more than thirty years now, and each year I reread it. I can quote whole sections, if called upon, but who would ever ask that. I realize now, that these works—the novels and stories I've been reading for over forty years—are the furnishings of my mind, so that when I read a novel such as *Mrs. Dalloway*, it is like entering a house where I have been many times, a place where I am unthinkingly at home.

I am no longer young, but I have been young, and have clear memories of what that felt like. This is the huge advantage of getting older, you have knowledge of both states. I look at my students, or for that matter my own daughter, who is now in her late twenties, and remember what it was like to be their age. But she could never imagine what it would be like to be mine. I remember the curiosity that made me quiet as I watched Stone on the day he died and remember too with something like amazement the hard-heartedness I showed that day.

. . .

I always begin my lectures on early-twentieth century literature with an explanation of the First World War and when I do, I think of Professor Coburn and Stone, who have strangely melded in my imagination over the years. I try to impress on the students what it meant for young people their age—the age Stone would have been when he went to war—to have the burden of wartime memories. These students, with their sprawling limbs overriding their chairs, their attention snapped away by anything but what I was saying at the front of the class. They'd look away, daydream, or take rushed notes. *This is important*, I want to say, *this is the way you can survive the bleakness not only of an age but when your life itself sinks into despair.* I want to tell them the angst they're feeling, that thing inside them that makes their view of me cloudy, that makes them slouch into the room, and encloses them in the gloom of their young years, that this situation is in full bloom in these writers we will together be studying. The air they breathed was the saddened atmosphere only known after a huge tragedy. *And look*, I want to say, *look, how they changed it into art.*

. . .

I'm reaching the age when I will stop teaching, when I will think of being less in the world and more in my own being. And I know when my students, with their disparate styles, look at me they see someone set by expectations, with my trim, sleeveless dresses, hair in a blonde bun, streaked now with grey that matches the blue-greyness of my eyes, high heels and poppy-red lipstick.

They would not believe my story of Stone, or rather to believe it they would have to modify the idea they have of me and see me as a young woman. And really I don't want them to. What has become clear over the years is that those months at Winter Willow were a time I can look back on and see how it joined who I was before with who I was to become.

## 22

I read in the paper ten years ago that Celeste died in a nursing home, one of the better facilities in the city, paid for, no doubt, by the generous inheritance left to her by Stone. The obit said she left behind a sister, nieces and nephews. I had never known she had a sister, and when I read that, I thought about the hours we had spent at Winter Willow together, how she may have been writing her sister in her room alone at night as I read upstairs and Stone slept, roamed the hallways or visited the third floor. She had gone to this nursing home from the hospital after Stone's death.

A few days after she was admitted when I went to see her there, I was told she wanted no visitors. So for the remaining years of her life—almost twenty—she lived a quiet, complacent existence, or so I imagined. But I also imagined that there were times when she would revisit that old house, in her thoughts, or dreams, or imaginings, revisit Stone, and Winter Willow would appear still and quiet, paralyzed in a snowy moment perhaps. I say this because I too can feel there is a space inside me where the thought of that winter season rests. In the final analysis, as I approach the age that Celeste was when I first met her, it seems that there is much that links us.

I remembered one Sunday during those winter months, drifting down sleepy to the kitchen and Celeste was standing by the back door that looked out to the garden. She did not realize I was there, and she was tapping on the window—tap, tap, tap—with her long

fingernail, its tiny sound filling the space between us. I stopped mid-
yawn, and saw that she was summoning a tiny sparrow that was
sitting by the back door on the parched branch of a rosebush that
would grow glorious in spring. She made a *tut-tut* sound and laughed
lightly when it flew away. It seemed to me on the day I read her obit,
that it was a good, a true thing, to remember her the way she had
been on that morning, alone and content, that it was my personal
eulogy for her, one that would never be shared, and yet marked her
life with an acknowledgment of a certain, common compassion.

. . .

After all these years, there is an image that returns to me from those
winter months, an image from the day I met Stone in the garden
behind his house. The air is sterile with an icy clarity except for the
fog that boils in slowly revolving banks, like thick ringlets of smoke.
I am a disruption to the white tissue of freezing air as I walk along
the pathway through the fog. The garden itself seems touched by the
silver grey of a frozen glove, flower stems bend from the weight of
snow, close in on the death of their blooms and the trees shimmer
with an icy glitter. The light is filtered through diaphanous layers
of fog, so that I cannot see where the path ends—there is only the
whisper of the shed's outline that comes into view and that weep-
ing winter willow, the tree the house was named after. I can see the
scene momentarily but then all is consumed by fog again. And Stone,
whom I do not see, stands by the shed, the tree drooping beside
him, his attention drawn to the woman I am at that moment and of
whom he has only caught glimpses as the fog clears and then returns.
What would he think the first time he sees me? A tall, blonde woman,
a woman with the appearance of his first wife, young, as she had
been when they married in the early twentieth century. How is
it possible that such an apparition appears to him on that day, in
that cold, still morning, when he is contemplating the fact of his
approaching death?

I am not sure, but what I do know is that the image of Stone from that day is an image I keep dear, for when the distance between us clears of fog and I am able to make out his form, for a reason I cannot fathom, I run toward him in my imagining, desperate to be held—something he'd never done and something I'd never wanted. I feel the angular sharpness of his thin form under my hands and feel his arms around me. As he speaks, I feel too the warmth of his breath and my hair tickling my ear. This close to me, without my being able to see his expression, he whispers, "I told you, Melanie. I told you spring does not always come."

I began to recall this moment during the summer my daughter had left to live with Martin, that summer I was alone for the first time in more than twenty years, when at night, I could not sleep. In the past I had not thought often of the season I lived at Winter Willow, but in the years since, the view of that garden and Stone standing at the end of the path, the still and icy image of him before the constant white of sky, returns at night when I close my eyes, curl around this life I have made, and fall into a warm sleep.

# Acknowledgments

I am indebted to Isabel Huggan for her help in the creation of this novel. Her gracious, sympathetic and skilled attention was invaluable, as is her friendship and I thank her for both.

For their unfailing support and sustaining friendships, I thank Frances Boyle, Laurie Koensgen, Jean Van Loon, Lise Rochefort, Jacqueline Bourque, Claudia Radmore, Doris Fiszer, Mary Lee Bragg, Rhonda Douglas, Mary Borsky, Kathlyn Bradshaw, Barbara Sibbald, Vicky Bell, and Una McDonnell. For his long-distant support, my gratitude to Ian Colford. For careful reading of the manuscript in an early version, my appreciation and thanks to Sonia Tilson. To the Ruby Tuesday writing group: I have come to depend on your encouragement, support and camaraderie—you are gems of the best sort. How fortunate I am to know such talented writers. And a special thanks to Natalie Taylor for her editing assistance with an early version.

I offer heartfelt thanks to my wonderful publisher, Enfield & Wizenty. I also wish to acknowledge the insight and wit of Ingeborg Boyens, my editor, who made working on the completion of this book such a pleasure.

I would like to acknowledge the blessing of my family and friends, who with encouragement and kindness, support me through the joys and tribulations of the writing life.

And to my first reader, André Savary, who has been there through it all, endless love and gratitude.

Thanks for the dream, Sis.

Literary works from the early twentieth century that supported the writing of this book are too numerous to cite, but I would like to note the following two books: Bill Goldstein, *The World Broke in Two: Virginia Woolf, T.S. Eliot, D.H. Lawrence, E.M. Forster and the Year that Changed Literature* (Henry Holt and Company, N.Y., 2017) and Stefan Hertmans, *War and Turpentine*, (Pantheon Books, N.Y., 2016).

I gratefully acknowledge the financial support from the City of Ottawa and the Ontario Arts Council.